TWELVE MONTHS TO WIN

THINGS WORTH TO WIN

" Mr. ' X ' steered slowly towards the yacht."   (Page 190)

TWELVE MONTHS
TO WIN

BY

JOHN F. C. WESTERMAN

WARD, LOCK & CO., LIMITED
LONDON AND MELBOURNE.

MADE IN ENGLAND

Made and Printed in England by C. Tinling & Co., Ltd.
Liverpool, London and Prescot.

CONTENTS

CONTENTS

CHAPTER I

THE MISSING FUNDS

" HELLO, Philip, old son! I was wondering if I should meet you on this 'bus!" exclaimed Robert Saye, leader of the Widgeon patrol, catching sight of Philip Hislan, the leader of the Bulls, the second patrol in their troop—the 28th Portlip—as he arrived on the top deck of the corporation vehicle. "I guessed you'd be coming along somewhere about this time."

"A simple bit of deduction, considering we are due at the hall at 7 p.m., with a ten minutes' journey from here, and 'buses only running every quarter of an hour!" responded his chum. "What's the news, if any?"

"Bad!" came the laconic response, as Saye seated himself and straightened out the top of his Scout's hat that had been flattened by the roof of the 'bus as its wearer had incautiously straightened himself at the top

7

of the stairs. Just six feet tall, the patrol leader of the Widgeons had to go carefully in low places, especially when the hat crown added inches to his stature. Hislan was two inches shorter and luckier in such circumstances. " Bell 'phoned me a quarter of an hour ago. As you know, he drew fifty pounds out of the troop account this afternoon before the bank closed to pay for the camp equipment and other gear that we must have ; well, he went round to the club-room with it and stowed it away in one of the drawers—under lock and key—while he did a few jobs. After a bit he happened to be by a window and saw a small boy knocked down by a cyclist. Naturally he dashed out with some first-aid kit, bandaged the kid up—he was pretty badly cut and bruised—and took him to his home just round a side street. So far so good, but when he got back to the club-room, finished off his work, he went to the drawer to get the cash and found it was missing. That would be about an hour later, from what he says. He immediately communicated with the police (having made absolutely certain that the stuff had been stolen) reported the loss and gave them the numbers of the notes, which he had, of course, noted—they were all fivers. The police have been to the room and looked for clues, but there's absolutely nothing, not even finger-prints on the drawer, except Bell's, and the lock was opened by a key, although Bell had the proper one in his pocket all the time. That's the news, old son—bad enough, isn't it ? "

" By Jove, yes," assented Hislan. " It will just about knock our camp on the head, I guess. But why did Bell draw the cash ? Wouldn't a cheque have done just as well ? "

" Not in the circumstances," explained his chum. " You see, his father is sending a lorry up to London to-morrow, so Bell was going to go with it, call at the Scout Shop, choose the stuff, pay for it on the spot and bring it all back on the afore-mentioned lorry. It was a chance too good to be missed and he didn't want to be hung up by a cheque. No doubt they would have accepted it all right, but there might have been a hitch. Mr. Wayte agreed and sent the signed cheque to Bell this morning. He is coming back himself to-night, but it would have been too late to cash it in the morning as the lorry leaves at 6 a.m. I was going along, too."

A*

"I see," acknowledged Hislan. "What a muck-up it has turned out. Some blighter must have taken advantage of Leslie being out bandaging that kid and nipped in to clean up the cash. Whoever it was must have had his eye on it all the time since Les left the bank. Well, it can't be helped now; we shall have to make the best of it and forego our camp for this year at least—I suppose there's not enough cash left to wangle a scratch equipment, or something?"

"Not a hope," responded his chum. "There's only an odd pound or two, and don't forget that money represented every penny the troop could scrape up since it was formed eighteen months ago, not counting the rent of the club and the cost of our uniforms, etc. Any other cash we have was to go in travelling expenses and catering for the camp, and we only had just enough for that. Still, here we are at the club. Come on!"

The pair got to their feet as the 'bus started to slow down and made for the stairway at the back.

"I'm sorry, sir!" apologised Saye, as he accidentally kicked the foot of an elderly, grey-haired gentleman, wearing plus fours, who was occupying a seat immediately behind theirs, as he moved.

"Don't worry, my fault!" came the reply. "Good luck to you!"

As he hurried after Saye, Hislan suddenly stopped, raised his hand in the Scout's salute, then followed his chum. "I say!" he exclaimed, as the pair alighted from the vehicle. "Did you notice that gentleman give the Scout's sign? He had the first three fingers of his hand stuck out on his knee, and he returned my salute when I made it."

"I didn't," admitted Saye. "I was too concerned about the hack I gave him. But I did see that he had a topping dog with him— it was between him and the window, on the floor. I was so busy looking at the animal that I didn't see his foot."

"I saw the dog, too," replied Hislan. "However, there's more important things to see to now. By Jove! the police are still hanging round," he added, as the pair entered the club-room and saw a constable and plain-clothes detective standing by the rifled desk.

"I must ask you young gentlemen to keep away from this corner," stated the detective. "At least until I have completed my investigations. Have either of you been here before to-day ? "

" No," replied the Patrol Leader of the Widgeons, giving his name and his chum's. " I only heard the news half an hour ago by telephone—I was at school all the afternoon and did not get home until after five o'clock. So was Hislan ; he's at the same school and in the same form as I am."

" Did either of you know that this money that has been stolen would be in this room this afternoon ? " was the next curt question.

" No," came the instantaneous response. " As a rule the place is deserted until the evening as we are at school. I was quite surprised when Bell rung me up and told me that he had been here this afternoon."

" Did you know that the money was going to be drawn from the bank to-day ? "

" I did," assented Saye. " At least I knew it would be if the cheque had been sent to Bell by the Scoutmaster, Mr. Wayte, to-day. I was to accompany Bell to London to-morrow to buy the camping gear we want. I have special permission to be away from school then."

The detective nodded. " So I have heard

from your friend, who, I believe, is the secretary of the troop," he acknowledged. " Now, can I verify your statement regarding your movements this afternoon ? "

Saye felt himself blushing. He realised that the man held him in suspicion because he knew that the money was to have been drawn from the bank that day, but his blushes were because his word was being doubted. A keen Scout, he paid strict attention to Rule I of the Scout Law—" A Scout's Honour is to be Trusted." " I gave you all particulars on my unspoken word of honour," he stated quietly, holding his temper. " Still, if you wish for verification, I can only refer you to my form-master at school—he will tell you I was there until four-thirty—and my parents, who will tell you I was home shortly after five. The intervening half-hour was spent in walking from school with Hislan here ; we both live at Capner and made a point of coming back together. In fact, we spend most of our spare time in each other's company."

" Oh, you do ? " The detective scribbled a few notes in his book. " And I am to understand that you accompanied Saye from school, both walking direct to your homes?" he asked, addressing Hislan.

"That is so," assented the Leader of the Bulls. "While you are checking my friend's statements, you can check mine at the same time, only referring to my parents for the last bit instead of his. There's one point, however, and that is that he came into my house for a few minutes at five o'clock to speak to my father. However, I should like to point out that it is hardly likely that we should take that money, as it was to be used for buying our camping gear, and was all contributed by the Scouts in this troop themselves. I don't know what lines you are working on, but I would suggest that you are wasting a lot of time in checking our movements. While you are doing all this the thief is getting well away. We want our funds back. Say the word, and we will do all we can to help the police run the guilty party to earth, but don't keep us answering questions about our movements. If you consider we cannot assist in any way, then let us get on with our work; we have a lot to do, and the rest of the fellows will be in directly."

The detective was slightly taken aback by the outburst for a second; then he recovered himself. "You are quite right in a way, Mr. Hislan," he agreed with a laugh, "but you must bear in mind that it is my duty to suspect every one for the time being. As for wasting time—well, my colleagues are busy outside while I check up everything I can in here. I shall not stay much longer, but I want to see everyone of your boys and your Scoutmaster, when he comes. What time do you expect him?"

"He should be here by eight o'clock," broke in Saye. "He has been away for a ten days' course at Gilwell Park and expects to get here by the six-thirty train, he told me. He said he would come round this evening to this place, as it is our regular meeting day."

"I see," responded the detective. "It's seven-twenty now, I notice. Will one of you stand by here and give me the names of each boy as he arrives, and a general description of his character? It is purely a matter of form."

"I'll stay," assented Saye. "Phil, you carry on with those reports, or chat with Bell about the state of affairs. See if there is any way of wangling enough gear for the camp and have all particulars ready to put to Mr. Wayte, when he comes.   We must try and get over the difficulty somehow."

" Bad luck for you if the camp falls through," remarked the police officer, as Hislan hurried away to carry out the orders of the senior patrol leader.   " It was to be your first, I believe ? "

" It was, and we were all looking forward to it," replied Saye.   " You see, we formed this troop a short while ago, Mr. Wayte volunteering to be our Scoutmaster, and decided to run it without any outside assistance in the way of funds.   We all have a pretty decent allowance in the way of pocket-money from our parents and turn in all we can of it to the troop funds.   Up to now we have done everything off our own bat—rented this hall, bought our uniforms and all the equipment we possess.   With this fifty pounds we were going to buy tents, a trek cart, blankets, cooking gear and other odds and ends necessary for camping and also, with the remaining cash, pay our travelling expenses and food bills for the camp.   We aimed at not costing our parents a bean for our holiday, but it seems

to be knocked on the head now. That's Jack
Raine, second of my patrol," he added, as a
youth of sixteen came through the door,
saluted smartly and passed quietly to the
other end of the big room. " Same school,
same form as myself, and a thoroughly good
man."

The detective nodded. " Good ! That's the
idea. I gather that these fellows won't have
heard of the robbery ? "

The senior P.L. shook his head. " Unless
they've seen it in the local paper," he stated.
" But I don't suppose they've had time to
put it in yet. George Wards," he broke off
again to name another newcomer. " Second
of Hislan's patrol. Same details as Raine.
In fact all our crowd are at Portlip Grammar
School, but in different forms."

The Scouts were arriving quickly ; it was
getting on for 7.30 — the time of assembly
for the troop — and Saye was kept busy
giving details of each lad as he appeared in
the doorway, saluted and passed down the
hall.

Punctually at the half-hour, the Senior
patrol leader excused himself to the detective
and blew his whistle. Immediately, the Scouts

stopped talking and moving about, awaiting orders.

" Troop.   Fall in ! " commanded Saye. " Raine ! Take charge of the Widgeons, as you did last week. Troop ! Alert ! "

The boys came smartly to attention and saluted as the Union Jack was slowly hoisted to a roof-beam.   Then they waited.

" Patrols will carry on with badge work until Mr. Wayte arrives," ordered Saye. " There will then be an important announcement.   I am leaving it for Mr. Wayte to make, but I can tell you to be prepared for bad news. You are prepared for it, so meet it with a smile when it comes.   Carry on ! "

As the Scouts began their work, he moved across to the secretary, who had resumed his interrupted task of reviewing the troop's depleted finances.   " What are the chances, Bell ? " he asked.

" Very slim—in fact, practically a wash-out," was the reply.   " As far as I can see at present, we shall have to either forego the camp or carry on with a bare minimum in the way of gear and get living and travelling expenses from our people, which is the very thing we decided we would avoid when we began this troop. What's more, we should have to lump the tents and other stuff on our shoulders, 'cos a trek cart is absolutely out of the question. I think the best thing we can do is to see what Mr. Wayte says about it when he comes. Bob, old man, I'm jolly sorry I was such a muff to lose that money. I wish to blazes I could make it up!"

"You couldn't help it, old son," Saye patted his friend on the shoulder. "You were only doing your duty in helping the injured and you haven't time to lock doors in circumstances like that. You did lock the drawer, and in nine cases out of ten that would have been safe enough. By sheer bad luck this was the tenth case. But what made you come back here this afternoon? You could have taken the cash straight home."

"I should have done so," admitted Bell. "But, you see, I wanted to find if there was a letter from the owner of Bos'n's Wharf giving us permission to camp there. Mr. Wayte told me that he had written and asked for the reply to be sent to me, addressed here. There was, and so I drafted out a reply, and began working out the best route to get there, and how much it would cost. In the middle of it all the trouble started. I had hoped to have all the particulars ready to submit to Mr. Wayte when he turned up to-night. I have—but they are no use now—and here he is ! "

The Group Scoutmaster—he was in uniform —paused at the door for a moment surveying the scene as he returned the P.L.'s salute. Although he saw the policeman and detective in his first glance, his face did not betray surprise or any other sign that anything unusual was taking place ; he merely waited until the senior patrol leader and troop secretary came up to him to report.

" Good evening, Saye ; good evening, Bell. Anything to report ? "

" Good evening, sir ! " returned Saye. Then, lowering his voice so that he would not be overheard by the other Scouts who were still carrying on with their work, he continued. " Bad news, I'm afraid, sir. The fifty pounds Bell drew this afternoon to pay for our gear was stolen from this room. He informed the police, who are investigating the case. As you can see, we have a detective and constable here this evening. I have not told the troop any news so far—I thought it best to leave it to you. Only Hislan, Bell and I know about it, apart from the police."

"Pretty serious outlook for our camp, then!" was Mr. Wayte's first comment. "But I'm glad the police are not here on account of any crime committed by our fellows, at any rate. I should like to hear your story Bell. Come over to the detective, introduce me and then fire away."

The Troop Secretary did as he was ordered and gave the Scoutmaster a detailed account of the afternoon's happenings, omitting nothing.

"That's the account he gave us, word for word, sir," stated the police officer. "We have the numbers of the notes and have taken the usual precautions, but we have failed to find any clues in here. The fact that this young gentleman here handled the drawer after the money was taken has put the matter of finding finger prints on it right out. I've no doubt he would have left it untouched if he had had any idea of a robbery, though! May I have a few words with you, alone, sir?"

"Just one moment, officer," requested Mr. Wayte. "Tell me, Bell, was the drawer locked when you returned to get the cash?"

"Yes, sir," was the reply. "I distinctly

remember giving it a pull before I felt in my pocket for the key. Then it unlocked without any trouble when I tried."

" Was there anything else in the drawer when you put the notes in it ? "

" No, sir. There was nothing in it at all until I put the envelope—it was the one they gave me at the bank—in it."

" Right you are, Bell; go and finish off your work while I have a few words with the detective. Now," he continued, turning to the officer, " what do you want to know ? "

For a good quarter of an hour the detective kept the Scoutmaster answering questions regarding the characters of the various members of the troop. He was able to say quite definitely that his boys were absolutely beyond suspicion. " In any case," he concluded, " Bell is the only one of them who handled the money, and at the time it went they were all at school. Of that I am certain. Bell had special permission to be away from school this afternoon, as you heard him say, and I'd willingly trust him with every penny I have in the world. I have found him honest to a fault—if one can use that expression—in regard to the troop funds, which he has handled since the beginning. I remember he kept working at the accounts until late one night because he could not account for one halfpenny on one occasion. It was eventually discovered by him that a letter had been over weight and the halfpenny had been used to make up the postage. I merely mention this to show you how careful he is."

" But he should have remembered that letter requiring an extra stamp," pointed out the detective.

" Not necessarily," objected Mr. Wayte. " As it happened, I took the extra stamp out of the stamp box and put it on myself. I did not mention it to him at the time, and forgot the incident until I was just about to go to bed. Knowing Bell was worried about an odd halfpenny, I 'phoned him at once, and the accounts balanced. Now, it's my turn to ask a few questions. Have you got the name and address of the cyclist that ran down the child, or anything like that ? "

" No, sir. He pushed off without waiting to see what damage he had done—must have been scared. We can't even get any reliable witnesses. Few grown-up people were about at the time, but a lot of small children were going home from school just then. The cyclist charged right through them, as far as we can make out. Naturally enough, all the interest was centred on the injured kiddie. Thanks to the prompt attention of your lad, I don't think he will come to any harm through it."

" It looks to me like a put-up job by at least a couple of men," commented the Scoutmaster. " I should say that they saw Bell draw the money from the bank, followed him here, watched him put it in the drawer and later created the disturbance to lure Bell out while one of them slipped in and took the notes. Unfortunately the lock on that drawer is only a common one and an average key of the same type would open it. The desk itself is old—I bought it for a few shillings in a junk shop—but as there was no lock on that particular drawer, I fitted one myself, just to serve to show that it was not to be touched by anyone but Bell and myself (we both have a key) more than anything else. The room and furniture belong to the troop, so any member can use anything in it, but that one drawer that I reserved for special things relating to troop business."

" Your theory of the robbery seems very

likely," agreed the detective. " It had occurred to me, too. Now, sir, I think I will be moving on; there seems little to keep me here just now. We shall get your money back before long, sir; you may depend on that ! " he added, reassuringly. " Good night, sir ! "

" Satisfied him at last, sir ? " asked Saye as the police officers left the room. " He seemed to suspect the whole crowd of us."

" I managed to persuade him that you were all to be trusted," replied Mr. Wayte. " In the end, to get rid of him, I gave him an idea to work on. Of course, he said he had already thought of it himself, but I doubt it," he added with a grin. " Come over to Bell with me; I want to see just what our position is regarding camp."

Rapidly the secretary put forward his facts and figures before the Scoutmaster until the latter knew all details regarding the position. Then he blew his whistle and ordered the troop to fall in.

" You have all heard that I have an important announcement to make and I am sure you all know that something unusual has happened, judging by the presence of the police officers until a few minutes ago," he began, when they had taken up their positions. "I am jolly pleased with your attitude—meaning your lack of inquisitiveness and quietness—although I'm sure you were all wondering what had happened.

"In brief, then, I'll tell you. This afternoon Bell drew fifty pounds from the bank to pay for our camp gear. This money was stolen from this room about an hour later while he was absent rendering first aid to an injured child outside. You must bear this in mind. There is absolutely no blame attached to Bell. He took precautions that would have been adequate in usual circumstances, but in this case they were not enough. It was not his fault, I repeat, and I am sure you will not even think of him being negligent.

"The loss of the money is serious enough, but we have another loss to contend with. I am referring to our camp. Without funds we cannot get the necessary equipment. The few pounds we have left in the troop's bank account are only sufficient to pay for our travelling and feeding expenses. We have already decided that the cost of this camp was to be met by the troop itself, so we cannot apply to anyone outside for money to meet the cost of gear without breaking our resolution. Much as I would like to, I cannot advance the necessary myself—my balance is somewhat depleted at the present moment, temporarily, I trust. Now, what are we to do ? "

Before anyone could say another word there was a sharp, imperative bark of a dog from the door.

" May I come in and say a few words ? " enquired a strange voice immediately afterwards. " I may be able to help you a bit."

CHAPTER II

MR. "X'S" OFFER

TURNING in the direction of the door, Mr. Wayte saw a tall, thickly-built, grey-haired gentleman, dressed in plus fours, standing in the half-opened door with an old English sheep-dog at his feet. The newcomer was a stranger to him, but Saye and Hislan instantly recognised him as being the occupier of the seat behind them on the 'bus over an hour before.

"Come in, sir!" invited the Scoutmaster, returning the Scout's salute that the gentleman made. "You belong to the Movement, I see?"

"Not officially, I'm afraid," was the answer, "although I did give you the Scout's sign. I am interested in the Movement, but do not take an active part in it—my spare time is somewhat limited. The only credential I can give you, I'm afraid, is this, although it is hardly suitable and looks like self-advertisement." The stranger fumbled in his pocket and produced a small gold Swastika-shaped pendant, on which was mounted the ornamented arrow-head of the Scout's emblem. Immediately all present recognised it as a Thanks Badge, and knew that its owner had received it for some services rendered to the Movement.

" Very pleased to meet you, Mr. . . . ? " exclaimed the Scoutmaster, extending his left hand. " That little emblem makes you one of us right away! Can we do anything for you ? "

" Yes and no," came the response, as the gentleman returned the handclasp. " You can by not asking for my name, for a start, and listening while I blather away to you all for a few minutes. That's your part for the time being. Do you mind ? "

" Not at all, sir," replied Mr. Wayte, as he introduced himself. " We will help you all we can."

" Good! It won't take much of your time," acknowledged the gentleman. " Just over an hour and twenty minutes ago I was on a 'bus that passed this place and I could not help overhearing a conversation between two patrol leaders of this troop. I had no intention of eavesdropping, but the comparative silence of these modern vehicles run by the corporation and the close proximity of the seats made it impossible for me not to hear. Now I gathered that this troop was intending to go camping very soon—their first camp, in fact—but a bad snag had cropped up. The sum of fifty pounds, drawn from the bank this afternoon, had been stolen from this very room. This money was to have paid for all the camp gear and accessories and represented practically the whole of the troop's capital.

" Then I heard the last part of your address, as I stood at the door, Mr. Wayte, and all I can say is to repeat ' What are you going to do ? ' The troop has pledged itself to bear the cost of this camp out of its own pocket, and has been let down at the eleventh hour, all because one of its members did his duty by attending to an injured child in the road outside—a hard reward for a kindly action."

" Your question is easily answered, sir," replied Mr. Wayte. " There is obviously no alternative to giving up all ideas of going to camp this year. It is a pity, but we shall

have to make the best of things and pass the
time by having days out in the country—
within marching distance, of course—and get
our pleasure that way. We did that last
year and had quite a good time. Of course,
we are all jolly disappointed, especially as
we have got permission to camp at Bos'n's
Wharf, but we can't manage it if we stick to
our resolution—which we will—and refrain
from obtaining our expenses from the lads'
parents. Our resolution was to pay our own
way entirely."

" So I gathered on the top of the 'bus,"
acknowledged the gentleman. " An excellent
resolution, too. I only wish there was more
of that spirit in existence. But it makes my
task extremely difficult. I may as well tell
you of a resolution I made myself not very
long ago—on the top of that 'bus, in fact.
It was this : I admired the spirit in which
those two patrol leaders accepted their loss.
I could see that they were keenly disappointed,
but there was not a hint of censure passed on
the lad—Bell, I believe his name is—who was
responsible for the money, nor were there
any moans over their loss—and I can see
that the rest of you accept it in the same

manner. Good for you all; I notice that
you observe the Scout Law which says that
' a Scout whistles and smiles under all difficulties,' or words to that effect.

" Pleased with this demonstration—particularly with regard to the two in the 'bus, as
they were the prime cause of my idea—and
having an odd fifty or sixty pounds in my
pocket, I resolved to offer it to you all to
enable you to have your camp, but it would
appear that your resolution rather puts the lid
on my scheme, doesn't it ? " The speaker paused
and looked intently at the lads before him.

" It's extremely good of you, sir, but I
am afraid that your supposition is correct,"
replied the Scoutmaster. " The lads must
do it off their own bat, or not at all. I am
speaking for them, because I know they mean
to stick to their word, hard as it is to do so
in the face of your offer."

" That's what I expected," resumed the
unknown. " Consequently, I have been trying
to think out a way in which it would be possible
for me to assist you in getting your camp. It
seems very unfair that you should lose the
pleasure of a holiday under canvas on account
of a good turn to an injured child. We want

to help these Scouts get to Bos'n's Wharf,
don't we, Nan ? " he added, addressing the
sheep-dog that was sitting, keenly alert, at
his feet.

For answer the big, black and silver grey
dog lifted her head, gave a sharp bark and
reared up on her hind legs to place her fore-
paws on her master's chest.

" You see, she agrees, too," he continued.
" I very often go by her judgment and I
find it very sound ; she understands practically
every word I say. This is my plan. It rests
with you to decide whether you will accept
it or not.

" I have purposely refrained from giving you
my name or address ; you'll see why later.
This is the third Tuesday in July, isn't it ?
Very good. I propose to lend the troop fifty
pounds so that it can buy the necessary gear
for camping and will call here, at this place,
on the third Tuesday in July next year for my
money, plus five pounds as interest, which
I think you will agree is reasonable. I am
not a money-lender, by the way, and I should
only ask for an I.O.U. from the Twenty-
eighth Portlip Troop as a form of agreement.
I have not finished yet, though. I would add

B

some conditions. I will say now that I do not live in Portlip, or within fifty miles of it. I am very rarely in this place—once or twice a year at the most—and, furthermore, I am away from my home for many months in the year, wandering about England. But if any of you find out who I am and where I live within the next ten months—I am not going to give you any assistance in doing this, naturally enough—and brings the troop to see me at my residence, I promise you that I will do my best to entertain you for a few hours and renounce my claim to the capital —in other words, the fifty pounds. The interest I will collect on the specified day and, in the event of my losing the fifty pounds, I will hand the odd five pound note to the Imperial Headquarters of the Boy Scouts' Association as a donation to their fund. Another thing, I should like a copy of the list of gear you intend getting and will visit the camp at Bos'n's Wharf one day and check over the stuff.

" You see, I am not giving you the money ; I am lending it to you as an investment, but giving you a chance to earn it back by under-taking the task of establishing my identity.

I will only tell you all one thing as a clue; between forty and fifty years ago I was at Portlip Grammar School, where, I believe, all of you go now. You may, or may not, get something to work on from that, but I warn you there were over two hundred boys there at that time. Now, will you take it on ? "

" That is a question I cannot answer for the lads, although I know what my own decision would be, sir ! " exclaimed the Scout-master with a smile. " Excuse me one minute while I ask the boys themselves. Now, the Twenty-eighth ! " he turned towards his troop. " You have all heard Mr. . . . , I mean this gentleman's generous offer. Bear in mind the conditions and remember that if you fail to establish his identity within ten months from now you will probably be camp-less next year for lack of funds again, unless the police recover our lost money. Take that risk if you will, and decide whether the acceptance of this offer is allowable under the terms of your resolution. I will give you all two minutes in which to decide. Patrol leaders, collect each lad's vote when I give the word and report the result to me ! "

Before the two minutes had elapsed the two

patrol leaders approached the Scoutmaster, and spoke a few words in low tone. Then Mr. Wayte turned to their guest.

" The troop wishes me to express its profound gratitude and says that your offer is accepted with their deepest thanks. But the Widgeon patrol wishes to know if they may use any means they like to establish your identity and address."

" Excellent ! " The gentleman beamed on the troop as he heard the decision. " Excellent. But no thanks, please. I am pleasing myself as much as you—bear in mind that I never do anything of this nature unless I want to. You may use any means you like to track me down—if you can. I shall not assist you in any way, as I said before. Now, I will hand Mr. Wayte the cash—I have changed it into one pound notes, you will observe, in order to cover my tracks—and he will give me the I.O.U. That will settle the matter."

Producing a vast bundle of notes from his pocket, the gentleman carefully counted out fifty of them into the Scoutmaster's hand. Then Mr. Wayte wrote out the I.O.U. which was signed by himself, Bell, as Secretary, and the two patrol leaders. Then Saye handed the paper and a fountain pen to the gentleman. "Will you sign too, sir?" he asked.

For an instant the unknown made as if to take the pen, then he pulled himself up with a jerk. "You nearly had me that time, my lad!" he acknowledged with a laugh. "Better luck next time, though! I might get caught in a moment of mental aberration!"

"I took the chance, sir; you said we could use any method we liked," explained Saye. "I've seen it done successfully before, but I reckoned you would have tumbled to it."

"Thank you," came the reply. "There's nothing like making a start at once in a case like this. By Jove! It's after nine o'clock! I must be making a move—I have a good two hours' drive before I get home, or rather more. You start camp the second week in August, I believe? Good. I will call on you one day. Good night all, and good luck!"

"Three cheers for Mr. 'X,'" yelled Saye, before anyone else could utter a word. The next moment the hall rang to the hearty response. Then with a hearty "Thank you all," the gentleman called his dog and departed amid a chorus of "good nights" from the Troop.

" Luck has been with you to-night," pointed out Mr. Wayte, as the door closed behind their benefactor. (He had prevented anyone seeing him off the premises with upheld hand.) " Thanks to the kindness of Mr. ' X,' as Saye described him — bearing in mind his algebraical problems, no doubt—you can have your camp. Furthermore, there is no need to put off the trip to-morrow to get the gear, Bell. Bear in mind that you have a chance of winning a clear forty-five pounds within the next ten months, but don't forget that, in the meantime, you have to raise fifty-five pounds in case you lose.

" Mr. ' X's ' offer is a sporting one. It is very obvious that he is not out for any gain himself, and his offer to cancel the debt was made to give you all a chance of getting the cash which your resolution prevented him from giving you directly. He wants you to win, I'm sure, but he is not going to give you any help—a very fair thing in the circumstances and, I consider, a compliment to your abilities as Scouts.

" Now, time is getting on and we shall have to pack up in a few minutes, but I have one more suggestion to make. It has just occurred to me. The fifty pounds is to be spent in buying the camping gear on the list Bell, assisted by Saye and Hislan, has made out, a copy of which Mr. ' X ' has taken with him. I do not know exactly what is on that list apart from the first section of absolute necessities that I checked over with them. That list must be adhered to, so there can be no saving up for payment day next year by cutting down the travelling expenses. Have you any suggestions for doing this ? Remember, I leave it in your hands."

" I have an idea, sir," replied Saye, almost at once. " You said that you were taking your car, I believe ? Well, I propose that the trek cart is towed by it to within a few miles of Bos'n's Wharf, where the Scouts who accompany you in your 'bus take it over and lug it to the camping site. With a bit of a squeeze you could get five aboard—one beside you in front, sir, one sitting on the floor at his feet and three in the dickey. They could lug the cart say five miles and then begin setting up the tents and all that. Then you could return and pick up another five from the crowd, who would be marching from here— or they could go a bit by motor 'bus and then begin hiking—dump them at the same place as the first lot and return for the rest. That would account for sixteen of us, counting yourself, and the remaining three could cycle the whole way. It would certainly mean a lot of driving for you, sir, but it would save the fares all right."

Mr. Wayte made a rapid mental calculation. " Yes, I think we could do that," he admitted. " It would take a long time, of course, and mean a good deal of marching for most of you. I don't think the police would object to the trek cart being towed by my car, provided it had a number plate stuck on the back. Right! Unless anyone else has a better suggestion, we will adopt that plan." He glanced up enquiringly. No one offered an alternative, and all expressed their approval of the scheme. " Very well, then," he continued. " It goes. But I think it would be better to increase the cyclists to six—three from each patrol—to avoid overcrowding in the car. Volunteers for cycling hand your names in to your patrol leaders before this time next week. Troop, alert ! Dismiss ! "

Stopping only to hand over the money to Bell and Saye, who took £25 each for greater

safety, Mr. Wayte hurried home. He had
had a heavy and exciting day and did not
want to keep the two lads hanging about
longer than necessary on account of their
early start for London the next morning, in
spite of the fact they tried to persuade him to
tell them of his experiences at Gilwell Park.
" I'll tell you all about it round the camp fire,"
he promised.

Shortly after six o'clock the following
morning, Saye met the lorry, with Bell on
board, on the main road for London, close by
his home. Swinging himself aboard as it
slowed down, he seated himself by his friend
and they began talking over the list of gear
they were to purchase, checking each item
from the catalogue and discussing its merits.
Then they turned their thoughts to the mysterious Mr. ' X.'

" We've simply got to find out who he is,"
observed Bell seriously. " I don't mean from
the point of view of getting the cash, Bob,
although I'll admit it means a lot to us, but
we must show him that we are capable of
performing the task he has set, if nothing else."

" You're right ! " assented the P.L. " As
you say, Les, the honour of the Troop is at

stake, as it were. From the other point of view it's necessary too ; we must have enough cash for next year's camp and other ex'es. It will take us a lot of doing to raise eighty or ninety pounds by this time next year—we should want quite that if we have to pay Mr. ' X '—and it's a tough proposition. We shall have to do it, of course, or run Mr. ' X ' to earth."

" There's always the chance that the police will recover our fifty pounds," pointed out the Troop Secretary. " But we must not count on that too much. Still, I have an idea. This Mr. ' X ' is coming to visit us at Bos'n's Wharf, isn't he ? "

" So he says," acknowledged Saye. " And I'm certain he will stick to his word."

" So am I, Bob. Now, remembering that the Wharf is five miles from the nearest station, how does this strike you ? " Leslie spoke rapidly for a few minutes.

" Might work," admitted Bob. " But you must remember that he is jolly astute, in spite of his reference to ' mental aberration ' last night. Besides, he might come some other way—by water, for instance."

" We shall have to take that risk, but we

might as well try the stunt when he turns up."

" Rather ! " came the reply. " We'll do it on our own—without saying anything to Mr. Wayte, I mean. You or I can't do it, but we might get one of the others away without his noticing it. It's a good scheme, Les, old boy. Ye gods ! we are nearly in London ! How the time has passed—and it's just after nine already."

Half an hour later—their pace was considerably reduced through the traffic-thronged streets of the Metropolis—they left the lorry at the foot of Victoria Street, impressing on the driver the necessity of calling at the Scout Shop in Buckingham Palace Road as near to noon as possible. " That gives you quite two hours to get your own stuff loaded," pointed out Bell. " And it won't take you that long," he added, wise to the working of his father's men.

The two hours in the Scout shop passed like as many minutes for the two lads as they selected tents, a trek cart, axes, cooking utensils, blankets, waterproof sheets, lanterns, buckets, rucksacks for each Scout, screens and the hundred-and-one odds and ends that were necessary for their camp. Besides two patrol tents, each capable of holding eight Scouts, they had purchased a small tent each for the two patrol leaders and a special one for Mr. Wayte—a surprise gift for their Scoutmaster, —who had been talking of borrowing one from one of his colleagues, if possible.

" That's the lot, thank goodness ! " exclaimed Bell, glancing from the huge pile representing their morning's buying to the solitary ten shilling note and small silver in his hand. " We would have been up a gum tree if we had discovered some essential thing was missing ! It has just worked out to a penny—this note I had put down as a tip to the driver of the lorry ; I think he will deserve it if he gets us home safely with this load ! "

Four o'clock that afternoon the camping gear was dumped at the Scouts' Hall and Bell handed over the note to the grateful driver.

CHAPTER III

FOR the next three weeks the troop **was** busy getting ready for the great day on which they were to make the trek to Bos'n's Wharf. Assiduously they practised setting up their tents and striking them, so that they would be able to undertake the task rapidly and neatly when it came to the real thing. Mr. Wayte's unexpected present in the form of the tent from his Scouts was a complete surprise to him, and he was extremely grateful to the lads for their spontaneous gift.

" Just one thing I wanted and needed to make me absolutely comfortable," he declared, when the presentation was made. " I had asked my friend if I could borrow his, but he was going camping at the same time ; as a result I was beginning to wonder how I could manage."

" A slight return for the use of your car,

not to mention all the work you have put in for us, sir," returned Saye. " We have already made a duplicate number plate to put on the back of the trek cart when you tow it," he held up an oblong piece of metal with the white numbers and letters glistening brightly—the paint was still wet.

" Excellent ! " came the reply. " You've made a good job of it, anyway. I shall know where to come when my number plates want doing again ! "

" Raine did these, sir," explained the P.L. " He's a past master at this sort of thing ; I'm sure he'd do the others for you when you want them."

" Rather, sir ! " acknowledged the Second of the Widgeons enthusiastically. " I'll do them before the camp if you like—they won't take long once the black background is dry."

" Thanks, Raine," returned the Scoutmaster. " But I'm afraid there's hardly time, just now. Perhaps when we get back from camp. By the way, speaking about towing the trek cart, I think it will be all right, provided we fix up some sort of brake on the cart to conform to the law. That is up to you. Any suggestions ? "

" That should be an easy job, sir," answered Hislan, who had been listening intently. " We could hang a balk of timber across the cart, just behind the wheels, and the fellows in the dickey could pull on a couple of ropes when braking is necessary, thus hauling the wood against the tyres."

" Hardly practical, Hislan, I'm afraid," objected Mr. Wayte. " You see, the tendency of the revolving wheels would be to throw the balk of wood upwards and would probably result in a total jamb against the springs and the pull of the two Scouts, working backwards from the dickey, would not be very effective in any case. Any more bright ideas ? "

" How's this, sir ? " asked Saye. " If Hislan's bit of timber is bolted to two wooden uprights, which are in turn secured to the body of the cart in front of the wheels and permitted to swing freely, there will be no danger of it running over or under the wheels. Then with a strong spring from the centre of the bar to the axle, say, to haul it against the tyres, you would have a fairly efficient brake."

" So far so good, Saye, but the brake would be clamped against the wheels all the time."

" Exactly, sir ; it would be an ' automatically-go-on' brake. To keep it off, we would have to have a light tackle—two single blocks should do—fastened to the centre of the timber brake and the iron loop under the cross bar on the handle. The end of the tackle would lead through the pulley farthest from the car and up to some simple sort of fixing in the dickey. All the fellows there would have to do on the word 'Brake' would be to let go easily. The spring would then clamp the wood against the wheels with a pressure varying according to the slackness of the tackle—the maximum being the full power of the spring. It wouldn't take much fixing or making up—two small bolts through the trek cart are all that's necessary there."

" That is a good idea," applauded Mr. Wayte. " See what sort of job you can make of it. You should be able to get hold of a good stout spring without much difficulty and the rest is just ordinary carpentry. When you have it finished we'll have a trial run, with unloaded trek cart. But we shall have to go jolly easily when we have that pile of stuff on it," he added, pointing to the large heap of gear that was stacked neatly in a corner of the hall. " 'Fraid it won't all go on the cart; each Scout will have to hump his share in addition, or we'll have to make two complete journeys."

"We'll manage it somehow, sir," the senior P.L. assured him. "Practically everything is there; we shall not get anything in the way of provisions here, we can buy them all at Redley. The only extra stuff will be our individual kit and each of us should be able to cart that in our rucksacks."

"That's so," affirmed the Scoutmaster. "But don't forget that the rucksacks will take up quite a lot of room in the car in each individual load. It will be a tight squeeze even without them."

"We could stow them on the running boards, or over the side, somehow," suggested Hislan. "They wouldn't hurt the paintwork if we shoved something over it first."

"We will have to see what we can do when the time comes," decided Mr. Wayte. "In any case, it wouldn't hurt the paintwork if we adopted your suggestion, Hislan," he added ruefully. "It's more than due for an over-haul—when the bank balance will run to it!"

"She looks jolly smart, all the same, and runs perfectly," averred Bell stoutly, referring to the car. " I wouldn't grumble if she belonged to me."

" I'll remember that when I want to sell her," promised the S.M. " I'll ask you for a written testimonial, Bell, or let you have her cheap ! "

" I may hold you to the last part of your statement, sir ! " threatened the Troop Secretary. " But in the meantime, sir, will you check through these papers ? "

" Right you are. But wait a moment, I see it's just on packing-up time. I'll dismiss the troop first," came the reply. " You stopping on, Saye and Hislan ? "

" Not to-night, sir," answered Saye. " Phil knows where he can get hold of a spring—or thinks so—and we are going to try and get it now, ready to make a start in the morning, now we have holidays." (For their school had " broken up " soon after the trip to London.)

" Very good," acknowledged Mr. Wayte. " The sooner the better ; time is getting short."

Ten minutes later, the troop having been dismissed, the two patrol leaders swung off at a steady pace to their destination.

" By Jove ! the water looks nice ! " exclaimed Hislan, as they passed along a path that bordered an arm of the vast harbour that gave their town its name. " I often wish we had a Sea Scout troop, yet we get oceans of fun out of ours."

" So do I," admitted his friend. " But, of course, you know Mr. Wayte is thinking of getting us a boat, the idea being that any of us who want to can learn a bit about seamanship."

" Yes, he spoke to me about it," replied Hislan. " He's going to look around after the camp for a suitable craft. He really wants it for himself, but is decent enough to offer us the use of it."

" He's a jolly fine Scout in all senses of the word," stated Saye decisively. " He gives us nearly all his spare time and has offered us practically everything he has that is likely to be useful to us. I only wish . . ."

He amazed his chum by breaking off suddenly, throwing down his Scout's hat and racing madly forward. Then, reaching the edge of the low sea wall that bordered the path on which they were walking, he took a magnificent " header " into the water and swam vigorously towards a long, dark, partially submerged object, that Hislan instantly recognised as a capsized dinghy, about 100 yards out.

Deliberately picking up his chum's hat, the leader of the Bulls ran to the same taking-off place, removed his own boots, hat and shirt, and in turn plunged into the sea. Arriving at length on the scene—he was not such a powerful swimmer as Saye—he saw that his friend was diving repeatedly, while a small boy of ten or twelve was clinging to the waterlogged boat.

" Small girl ! " spluttered Saye, as he came gasping to the surface and making a downward jerk with his thumb. " Can't find her ! "

Simultaneously the two Scouts dived through the discoloured water and swam round under the surface with half-bursting lungs. Then, together they saw a dim white object beneath them and, with their hearts pumping with deep thuds under the strain they forced themselves still further down, until their hands grasped their objective almost together. It was the unconscious form of the child.

At the surface again, they drew in great breaths of life-giving air and looked around. Thank goodness the small boy was still clinging to the boat and, with a nod to his chum, Hislan released his hold on the girl and swam to the boy and induced him to release his hold and permit himself to be towed ashore, while Saye performed a similar service to the girl.

Short as the time had been, it was sufficient for a fairly large crowd to gather on the bank, but no one offered to help the burdened Scouts as they struggled through the water, save by cheers. Even a boat moored close at hand was ignored, although it would have helped the semi-exhausted P.L.'s. as they kicked out as vigorously as they could. Clothed as they were, the sharp dash to the scene of the accident and the diving for the children had sapped their strength considerably.

Willing hands assisted them up the wall to the path above, and without loss of time the two Scouts, puffing like steam-engines on a long up-grade, applied artificial respiration to the small girl, bidding the onlookers stand back and fetch a doctor as they worked, while a woman took charge of the boy and hurried him homewards at their curt order.

Ten minutes later, just as the child was coming to, the doctor arrived on the scene and, after a few words of commendation to the still busy lads, took over the work.

" Now's our chance ! " hissed Hislan, as he retrieved their trodden-on hats, and his own shirt and boots. " Get away before there's any awkward questions."

" Yes, home as quickly as we can ! " returned Saye, his teeth chattering as the light breeze cut through his sodden clothing. " You have at least got a dry shirt, you lucky blighter ! "

" Yes," admitted his chum, as they jogged off at a smart pace to keep dry. " But I clean forgot to take off my watch—it's done for, I'm afraid."

" So's mine, Phil, old man, but that isn't very serious, in the circs. We were lucky to get away before the police turned up and made enquiries. We shan't be wet enough to notice by the time we get home, that's one thing. Come on. Your best foot forward ! "

Luck was with them that night, for each

was able to get home and change without any awkward questions being asked, but in the morning newspapers was a long account (supplied by an eye witness) of how two Scouts, who eventually slipped away without giving their names, gallantly rescued two children from drowning after a small boat they had accidentally untied while playing in, had drifted away and upset. A fairly accurate description was given of how the two Scouts had dived many times to find the girl and of their work of artificial respiration on the bank, afterwards and the story finished with a statement that it was known that the "brave lads" were from the 28th Portlip Troop of Scouts, an onlooker having read the name on the shoulder-strap of one of the Scout's shirts.

"Is this the reason why your shirt, shorts and stockings are soaking in a bucket of water under your bed this morning?" demanded Mrs. Saye, pointing to the account and eyeing her son accusingly. "You might have told me last night and I could have sent those clothes to the laundry."

"I didn't think of that," stated the P.L., avoiding a direct answer for once.

"Never mind, dear, I'm prouder of you than I can say," she responded. "I suppose Philip was the other lad mentioned: I must 'phone Mrs. Hislan and warn her to look to his clothes too. I'll fix yours up myself— I'll soon wash them out. I know you'll be needing them in a hurry for your camp."

"Don't say anything about it, Mother," begged her son. "Neither Phil nor I want a fuss about it."

"I shan't make a fuss, you silly boy; but don't think you won't be located by the newspaper men; they'll soon find out who you are, especially the local reporters!"

She was right; five minutes after Hislan arrived to take his chum round to get the spring that had been the object of their quest the previous evening, a reporter from the *Portlip Star* knocked at the door and requested an interview.

"Someone to see you, Bob, and Philip too, I expect," announced Mrs. Saye, who had received the newcomer with an "I-told-you-so" smile. "I've shown him into the morning room."

"Mr. Robert Saye, I believe," said the newspaper man, addressing Bob as he entered the room with his chum. "And Mr. Philip Hislan, if I'm not mistaken?"

"Quite right," assented Saye. "What can we do for you?"

"I represent the *Portlip Star*," came the reply. "I would very much like to have your accounts of your plucky action last night when you two pulled those children out of the water."

"First of all, how did you find out that it was us?" asked Hislan. "We purposely tried to keep it quiet."

The reporter smiled. "Things like that can't be kept quiet in a town like this, especially when some of our own citizens were involved and a number of others saw the whole thing," he pointed out. "I quite appreciate the fact that you wanted just to fade out and hear nothing more about it, but, you see, it is my job to ferret these things out. In this case, it was very easy. Several people noticed you were from the Twenty-eighth Portlip Troop and all I did was to visit Mr. Wayte, your Scoutmaster. I must confess he was not very willing to talk at first, but I managed to get the information from him that you two had left the Scouts' Hall at nine o'clock last night. I had already heard a rumour that the two rescuers were wearing patrol-leader stripes on the left-hand pocket of their shirts and allowing for the time taken to reach the scene of the accident, it wasn't very difficult to pin the solution to you two. So, having got your address, I came along at once. Now, what about your story ? As a favour to a brother Scout—I was in the Fourth Portlip Troop many years ago—you might make it exclusive to the *Star*. What do you say ? "

The chums assented. After all, they decided, it was better to have a true account published than leave it to the journalist's imagination. The fact that he knew their names completely destroyed all their hopes of evading publicity in the " local rag," and the fellow was a brother Scout, as he said.

That afternoon their plain and unvarnished story of the rescue, embellished by other facts the reporter had learned regarding the troop, was published in a prominent position in the *Portlip Star* under heavy type headings that read : " QUEST FOR SPRING SAVES LIVES OF CHILDREN." " PLUCKY SCOUTS DIVE FOR

GIRL IN HARBOUR." There was also a reference in the editorial to the good work performed by the town's Scouts and the excellence of the Movement's activities. But luckily for them, Bob and Phil managed to suppress the reporter's desire to secure their photographs for printing, yet they were recognised several times during the next few days when they appeared in uniform, much to their disgust.

Knowing their dislike of attention, Mr. Wayte had merely pressed their hands in a hearty and knowing manner when they had turned up at the hall that afternoon, complete with the spring—that was ideal for their purpose—and muttered "Good lads!" But it meant much more to them than anything else he could have done or said.

That was not quite all that arose out of the incident, however, at the time, for the following morning there was a letter, bearing the postmark of a little village a few miles off, addressed to Mr. Wayte at the hall. There was no address on the top of the sheet, merely the date, and read: "Dear Mr. Wayte, with great pleasure I read an account of a plucky rescue effected by Patrol Leaders Saye and Hislan of your Troop in the *Portlip Star* this evening. As a result I wish more than ever that I could give the Troop a hint as to my identity and wash out the loan, but regretfully recognise that it would not be playing the game in the circumstances. I will say one thing, though. I do not live here at Immering, I am merely passing through in the course of my wanderings. Yours, Mr. 'X.'"

"I'm glad he's pleased, anyway," remarked Saye, as he turned away to finish bolting the improvised brake after "knocking off" to hear the Scoutmaster read the letter. "There now, that's finished; we've only got the tackle to fix up before it's complete. When can we have a test with the car, sir?"

"This afternoon, two-thirty sharp," came the response. "Will you have it ready by then? I'll bring the 'bus along and we'll try it on a short run, say to the top of Down Hill and back. That will be more than we shall have to negotiate in getting to Bos'n's Wharf, anyway. By the way, I think we should have a light load on the cart to keep it steady, after all. The folded canvas of the tents and poles should be enough, I think."

" Thanks, sir. I'll have it ready," promised Saye. " This thing will just about lock the wheels when it's hard on, I should think," he added, giving the cart a push and not moving it against the pressure of his contraption as he spoke.

That afternoon the test was carried out successfully. After one or two attempts and a few minor adjustments the work was passed as O.K. and the " brake crew " fairly well drilled in their task as they sat in the dickey seat, " under service conditions," as Hislan expressed it.

The next three days passed quickly as the troop made their final preparations for their camp, working hard to get their equipment and gadgets ready to time, for they found there were endless details to get fixed up to avoid any possibility of any necessary object —big or small—being left behind.

" Troop, fall in ! " ordered **Mr. Wayte**, at the close of the last evening before departure. " You will parade here to-morrow morning at nine-thirty, with all your kit, ready for the camp. We hope to get moving by ten-thirty. Each Scout will bring his own lunch, and all being well, we shall all have our tea together in camp in the afternoon. Patrol Leader Hislan will take charge of the marching party; Second Leader Raine, the cycling detachment, and Patrol Leader Saye will look after the trek cart squad, which will be dumped by me five miles from Bos'n's Wharf as soon as possible. The cyclists will join them as soon as they can and I will make as many runs as are necessary to pick up the hikers. The latter party will tell me to-morrow if they intend to travel part of the way by 'bus or not—it's up to them. That's all, I think. You all know what kit you have to bring—but make it as little as possible—and don't forget the essentials. Dismiss ! "

CHAPTER IV

THE CAMP BEGINS

PUNCTUALLY at 9.30 the following morning the troop paraded in full uniform and kit. It seemed impossible that so much gear could be accommodated on the trek cart and on the Scouts' backs, but an hour's steady and unhurried packing saw the last of the equipment safely stowed and the cart was run out of the hall and secured to the back of the car, its load lashed tightly and compactly in its body and an old blanket taking the rub of the drag pole on the paint work of the two-seater.

Swiftly the cyclists and hikers moved off, the latter to a 'bus stop from where they had decided to get a " lift " for the first six miles into Dareham, from which place they would leave the busy main road and traverse quieter byways for a considerable portion of their journey. Then the remaining four Scouts

—Saye, George Wards, the second of the Bulls, Roy East of the same patrol, and Bell —packed themselves into the two-seater with Mr. Wayte and moved off at a modest 15 m.p.h. through the busy streets of the town, Bob taking personal charge of the brake rope and the trek cart's iron tyres clattering noisily over the metalled roads as it lurched after the car.

" Now, lads, we have every bit of thirty miles to cover before we reach Bos'n's Wharf on the first journey," remarked Mr. Wayte, as they drew clear of Portlip. " I think I should be able to dump you just before noon—the cart seems to be standing this speed all right ; we're doing twenty. The hikers will reach Dareham by about eleven and will be nearly four miles out by the time I drop you. Barring accidents I should be able to pick up the next batch about one o'clock. Meanwhile the cyclists should reach camp by one-thirty to two. Four o'clock should see us all settled. When you get to the ground, begin preparing the layout as I showed you and get your tents up. You can leave mine until I get there myself."

" Very good, sir," responded Saye, who was listening and speaking from the dickey over the folded hood. " Shall we get the food in the meantime ? "

" That's the idea," responded the S.M. " Bell has a list that will carry us through the first day and following morning. As the others turn up to help, some of you can run into Redley and get it, or, if you like, you can buy it on your way through."

The run was pleasant through the fresh countryside and, although care was necessary when driving through villages and towns, the brake party found themselves with little to do. All too soon for the Scouts Mr. Wayte pulled up and ordered them to proceed on foot with the cart.

" Well under five miles to go," he announced. " You know the way, Saye ? Good ! Don't rush it too much ; you have plenty of time and remember not to take up too much room on the road—a car might come round one of the corners suddenly, so ' be prepared ' as usual. All ready ? Then carry on and good luck ! "

Waiting a few minutes to see the party get well under way, Mr. Wayte turned his car and retraced his path at a smart pace, stopping only to exchange a few words with the cycling Scouts, who had made good progress and were a few miles in front of the hikers, who had covered the first ten miles by motor 'bus, and were, they reported, coming on well.

" You've a chance to surprise the advance party, if you feel like it," announced the S.M. " If the idea appeals to you, take the ferry at Outhampton across the water —it's only a few minutes' run—and it will save you a long ride, landing you within six miles of Bos'n's Wharf. The other way is quite double the distance. However, please yourselves. You can see the route on that road map you've got, anyway. I expect I'll pass you again before long. Cheer-oh! "

A quarter of an hour's run brought the Scoutmaster in touch with the remaining members of his troop. The Scouts were swinging along at a smart pace, but halted as the car drew up.

" Well, Hislan, how are things going? " he enquired.

" Fine, sir! " came the reply. " We have managed to do just four miles an hour since leaving Dareham; I've checked it by the milestones. No one has complained so far."

" Good. That's the spirit! Now, we must not waste time, or you will have further to walk. The three youngest Scouts and Second Leader Wards will now fall out and get in the car. All fit? Right! I'll be back for the remaining four of you as soon as I can. Mind you stick to the route I showed you, Hislan, or I might miss you. You may as well hand over your rucksacks; we will find somewhere to stow them and ease you on your march. Go steadily, mind! So long! "

Depositing his passengers within a mile of the camp—he had run them further than he had first intended as they had the extra rucksacks to carry for their companions— the Scoutmaster resisted the temptation to see how the first contingent were getting on in the camp and, having definitely ascertained that Wards knew the way to lead his little band, turned to make the last trip of the day. Just on two hours later the little two-seater bumped its way off the road, through a tree-studded track and came to rest in the clearing that had been chosen for the camp.

It was an ideal spot. Bounded on three sides by trees, the open space was roughly 150 yards in diameter, while on the fourth side ran the tidal Redley river. Fifty feet in from the water side there was a cutting, twenty feet wide and lined with rough pieces of timber, from which the place got its name.

Up to a hundred years previously it had been an important fitting-out berth for small coasting vessels, but had since fallen into disuse. Mr. Wayte had known of it for some years, although it lay well off the beaten track. He had visualised it as an ideal camping ground from his first glimpse of it, and he was right.

When the last members of the Troop arrived they found that the two patrol tents and two leaders' tents had been set up, fully fifty yards separating each patrol's quarters. Refuse and other pits had been dug, ready for use, and a cheery fire was burning near the partially-finished camp oven and, best of all at the moment, several billies of water were boiling ready to make tea. Within ten minutes all hands were sitting down to an early, but none the less welcomed meal.

It was after 6 p.m. before the camp was " squared up " to Mr. Wayte's satisfaction ; then the Scouts turned to and constructed a brushwood shelter over the car. They had obtained permission to cut wood from the copse surrounding the clearing and a plentiful supply of bracken from close by formed the roof and stopped the open chinks in the sides.

" What beds have you prepared for yourselves ? " asked the Scoutmaster, when the temporary garage was finished.

" Piled bracken, sir," responded Saye. " We have also put some in your tent—it seems dry and safe."

" It will make a comfortable bed," acknowledged Mr. Wayte. " But it will also make a beastly mess if it is only piled. Turn each patrol to to make proper camp mattresses. It won't take long and you will consider the time well spent when you see what a lot of trouble it saved."

" How do we carry on, sir ? " asked Hislan, when the patrols had mustered.

His Scoutmaster looked at him keenly before he answered. " Philip, I am surprised at you," he remarked quietly. " I told you two ways last year. However, you'll soon get the hang of it once we start. We'll use the camp loom type, I think ; it is the more substantial way in the end. For a start, collect fifteen fair-sized stakes and bring them here. Three of them must be fairly long— three Scouts' staves will do admirably, so get a dozen others from the wood. Bell, you get that big ball of twine from the odds and ends bag and then we shall be ready to make a start."

The materials were forthcoming in a very short while, and, under Mr. Wayte's directions, two stakes were planted firmly in the ground 3 feet 6 inches apart. Across the top of them one of the staves was lashed securely. Next, at a distance of 7 feet on either side of the first structure, a row of five stakes was planted. Then the S.M. took the twine and put ten small loops on the cross bar of the centre stakes and, moving to the outside row on one side, he tied the end of the string to stake number one, brought it back and passed it through loop number one, retracing his steps until the string overlapped stake one by five feet. Then he cut it and made the second end fast to another Scout's stave that was lying parallel to the stakes, keeping the cord in line all the time.

" Now," he stated, " carry on putting strings to each stake like this one, but be careful to keep them parallel. The Bulls will do the same over the other stakes, using loops two, four, six, eight and ten to pass the strings through. The Widgeons will stick to the odd numbers."

Rapidly getting the idea, the Scouts swiftly rigged the cords and waited for further instructions.

" Bring all that bracken out of the tents," was the next order. " Now, the patrol leaders will take the two loose cross bars and hold them as high as they can with the strings taut. The others will then put a rolled layer of bracken in the angle formed by the strings. That's the idea ! Now, P.L's. put your beam down as low as you can. Scouts, another line of bracken under the five horizontal strings this time, and over the beam strings. Now, Leaders, up again and continue until the fern reaches the five uprights on each side. Got that ? Good. When you have finished, tie the ends round the last layer, cut away from the stakes and cast off the loops at the fixed cross bar and there you have good, comfortable, and tidy mattresses. Continue until you have one for each member of your patrol. The first to finish can do one for me ! "

Entering into the task with a zest, each patrol strove to beat the other and the pile of finished mattresses grew rapidly, despite the fact that four members from each side had to collect more bracken and ferns to cope with the demand. Luckily they grew in profusion quite close.

" Ten done, sir ! " called Saye, as he finished tying the last knot.

" Nine here, sir ! " echoed Hislan, desisting in the work of reeving a fresh line of strings, recognising the fact that the rival patrol had won and made an extra one for the S.M. " Do we require any more ? "

" Not to-night, at any rate," decided Mr. Wayte. " Leave the stakes as they are for the present ; we may need some screens to-morrow and we can make them the same way. There's just one more job that you have not done, though. I see there are some tall young saplings in the wood over there

Fell one neatly, strip it and set it up in the centre of the clearing here for the flag. Some of you get the pole, the others dig a hole for fixing it, but don't forget to secure the pulley to the top and reeve the halliards before you set it up. Quick as you can, now, and when you have finished it there will be a ten minutes' ' cooler ' before bathing parade ; I see the tide is up."

Cheers greeted the announcement and within a quarter of an hour the flagstaff was put in position. Then the Scouts obediently " cooled off " for the prescribed time before donning their swimming-kit.

" Saye and Hislan, put your coats over your shoulders and stand by in case anyone gets into difficulties," ordered the Scout-master, when they were all ready for the bathe. " You can have your turn when the others are out ; I know you are good swimmers. No one is to swim outside the dock—there's plenty of room for you there and you are safe from the tide. But mind the mud on the bottom ; it's inclined to be soft and sticky. You have a lifeline handy, Saye ? Good ! Now you have ten minutes —in you go ! "

c*

Laughing and shouting the sixteen Scouts plunged into the calm water, churning it into foam as they splashed around, the two patrol leaders looking on enviously. But they recognised the necessity for bathing picquets and, like true Scouts, waited patiently for their own turn, keeping a wary eye open on their companions the while. The Scouts were all good swimmers — Mr. Wayte had seen to that—but there was always a chance of the dreaded cramp attacking one of the lads, particularly after their strenuous day.

All too soon for the bathers, Mr. Wayte's whistle summoned them from the water, and, as the last Scout reached dry land, Saye and Hislan dived into the dock. It was significant of the true Scouting spirit that the two lads did not ask permission to swim out into the river, much as they wanted to, but they were not the type that show off their powers or try and take advantage over their fellow Scouts by reason of their superior positions in the troop. The dock was the official bathing pool and they stuck to it, Mr. Wayte himself standing by to see that they did not get into difficulties, while the others dried and dressed themselves.

Their allotted ten minutes up, the P.L.'s. hurried to their tents and dressed. Then, while the cooks were preparing cocoa, which, together with biscuits, was to form their supper, the remainder dragged their home-made mattresses to their tents and prepared their beds for the night.

Supper was finished and cleared away by 8.45 p.m., and, with the fire made up the Scouts sat round talking and yarning as the twilight deepened and the flickering flames threw a stronger light over the surrounding darkness. Each party gave a description of their journey as they reclined with relaxed limbs growing more tired as the minutes sped.

The cyclists were able to report an easy run with no trouble. They had taken the ferry as suggested and arrived fully half an hour before they were expected. This had proved a great help, however, for they had been able to lend a hand in getting the tents set up.

The hiking party also had no out-of-the-way occurrences to tell of, but Hislan stated that he, for one, was glad when his turn to get into the crowded car arrived. The other three who had formed the last batch agreed with him.

" We had quite a decent time," stated Saye. " Although the trek cart was a bit of a drag on any slight hills we had to climb. We stopped in Redley for a few minutes to buy the grub and turned to directly we got here. First of all we relieved the cart of its burden, sorted the stuff out and dumped it in its approximate positions. Then we got busy with the spades and dug the various pits, as per instructions, rigged up the screens and got wood to start the fire. As the others turned up we were able to proceed faster and just about finished as the car rolled up. Not bad going, considering all things, but I must say I feel jolly tired now."

" You have certainly laid out the camp well," acknowledged Mr. Wayte. " Still, I had no qualms about leaving it to you ; the models we made during the year gave you all a good idea of the work—that's why I gave you the tests. Well, it's just on nine-thirty and time to turn in. Lights out at

ten o'clock, remember. I'll look in each tent
before then to see that you are all fixed up
properly. Carry on ! "

Without any delay the weary Scouts made
for their tents. Many of them would get
little sleep the first night, the Scoutmaster knew, owing to the excitement and
the strangeness of their surroundings, but
he was certain that they would give no
trouble.

Retiring to his own canvas shelter, he made
sure that all the guy ropes were of the correct
tension, and got into his pyjamas. Then,
donning an overcoat, he entered the Widgeons
tent. The lads were all in their improvised
but comfortable beds, talking hard, but they
stopped directly he arrived and looked round
critically.

" Good ! " he exclaimed, as he saw that
all the discarded garments were neatly folded
and stowed away, yet handy in case of
emergency. " That's the idea. But, tell me,
has anyone looked to the tent guys ? "

" No, sir," was the reply.

" Then the senior man—that's you, Raine—
had better do it. There's no indication of
rain, certainly, but there is a heavy dew.

Unless the ropes are slacked off a bit you will find them pulling the pegs loose, or straining the canvas when they shrink, as they are bound to do. Remember that each night and don't forget to tighten them again in the morning, when they dry, or you'll have sagging tents. All O.K. ? " he asked, as the Second returned to his bed—he had made the lad do the job in order that it would not be forgotten in the future. " That's the idea. Now, I'll give one blast on my whistle at ten o'clock, and I want to see the lights go out at once. Good night ! "

" Good night, sir ! " came a chorus, as he slipped through the entrance, and let the flaps of canvas fall behind him.

His visit to the Bulls' tent and those of the two patrol leaders was a repetition of the first. In each case the Scouts had neglected to look to their guy ropes, but Mr. Wayte did not admonish them very much. It was their first camp, he remembered, and, although he had warned them about the ropes on several occasions, he bore in mind that they had remembered several details, out of which the one forgotten was small. In each tent they had prepared for rain by digging a small hole close to the foot of each pole, into which the butt end could be dropped to relieve the tension, he noticed, but they had not allowed for the dew.

Squatting patiently at the door of his tent, the S.M. waited for ten o'clock. Then, as the hands of his watch pointed to the hour and the chimes of the village clock just over a mile away began to sound, he blew a blast on his whistle and gazed at the tents. Then he gave a grunt of satisfaction —the lights, showing brightly through the canvas, were extinguished almost together and the chatter of conversation ceased as the lads composed themselves for sleep.

Then, rising to his feet, he strolled round the limits of the encampment, casting a critical eye over the ground. There was no cause for complaint, all was quiet and orderly.

Five minutes later the Scoutmaster got into his own bed. An old campaigner, he knew how to make himself comfortable. First of all he spread his ground sheet under and over his bracken mattress. Then he spread one blanket so that the major portion was along the left side of his bed. The second blanket was placed on top with the surplus on the right side. Then he stretched himself on top, placed his pillow in position and wrapped the spare piece of the top blanket round his body. Then the first blanket was wrapped round in the reverse way, and tucked in well. Two minutes later, the lamp out, he was fast asleep.

CHAPTER V

THE FIRST DAY AT CAMP

A FEW minutes before 7 a.m., Mr. Wayte stirred in his bed, awoke and glanced at his watch. Listening intently, he found that the camp was quiet; the Scouts were still asleep, but, according to the routine time-table, it was time they were aroused.

Slipping out of his blankets, he fetched a bucket of water, sluiced his head and shoulders and, donning his coat over his pyjamas, proceeded to call the patrol leaders. In less than five minutes the troop, with the exception of two Scouts forming a picquet, was in the water for an early swim, completely dispersing the last vestiges of sleep. Then, when dried, the cooks started their fires and heated water for their Scoutmaster's shave.

Dressing finished, the bedding was brought from the tents into the sunshine for airing and the tents themselves squared up and tidied, each patrol competing with the other in an effort to have its own portion of the camp more spick and span than the other. An hour swiftly passed and at eight o'clock Mr. Wayte blew his whistle and ordered the lads to fall in.

In obedience to a command, Second Leader Raine stepped from the ranks and, as the Scouts saluted, slowly hoisted the Union Jack to the top of the improvised flagstaff; then, when he had returned to his place, heads were bowed while the Scoutmaster recited a short prayer. A quarter of an hour later, amid the aroma of porridge, bacon and eggs and tea, the troop settled down to enjoy a hearty, well-cooked breakfast in the open air, each member tucking in with gusto.

Contrary to Mr. Wayte's belief, the Scouts had all passed a quiet night. They had been so tired by their exertions that sleep had overcome their excitement and the strangeness of their surroundings, nor had anyone awakened until called by their leaders. One and all had testified to the comfort of their camp-made mattresses.

Breakfast over, the task of washing and clearing up proceeded quickly, but it did not escape ¸ Mr. Wayte's notice that,ˊ following a few words from Saye, Bell slipped quietly away with one of the bicycles, but he did not say anything—he had full confidence in his senior patrol leader. Ten minutes later, the Troop Secretary returned, approached the S.M., saluted smartly and presented him with a newspaper and a bundle of letters that he had collected from the near-by village.

" Thanks, Bell," he acknowledged. " Any trouble in getting the mail ? "

" No, sir. The post office is the general store and the postmistress recognised me— I bought the stores there yesterday—and as the letters are all endorsed ' 28th Portlip Troop ' and she saw the same thing on my shoulder strap, she handed all of them over without any trouble."

" Good. That saves the lot of us going there one by one to get all our individual letters. If I had thought of it, though, I could have handed you a chit authorising you to collect the mail; however, it is not necessary, apparently. Thanks for remembering to get me a paper. Remind me to refund you the money."

"It was Saye's idea, sir," returned Bell, modestly giving the credit of the idea to his friend. "Will you give the letters out, or shall I?"

"You carry on with it, Bell. Do so each morning, it will save time. Hello! there's one for me—I didn't expect any. Warn the patrols there will be inspection in five minutes, will you, please?"

Directly on time, Mr. Wayte ordered each patrol to fall in by its tent, and, accompanied by Saye and Hislan, he carefully inspected each Scout and the four tents—into which the beds and bedding had been re-stowed —as well as the camp generally and the cook's gear. Then he ordered each patrol leader to march his patrol to the flagstaff.

"You have made a good job of things considering it's your first day in camp," he stated, addressing the troop. "But there is just one thing I want to see done in the future. In each patrol tent I notice that the blankets are not placed uniformly in the beds. Some are at the foot, some at the head and some in between. Place them all at the head of the beds in future—it makes all the difference to the neatness of the camp. Now, there is just one more thing. This morning I had a letter that is really for the whole troop. I will read it to you. It is merely headed ' Caernarvon,' and yesterday's date. It goes on: ' Greetings to the 28th Portlip Troop in camp at Bos'n's Wharf. May the days be happy ones. I will visit you all within two or three days of your receiving this letter and meanwhile wish you all happy scouting. Mr. ' X '.'—You will see that he intends to carry out his promise and see us under canvas, so it will be up to you all to entertain him well. I know I can rely on you to do this.

" Before I dismiss you there is one other thing. This morning is to be devoted to Scouting practice. I am leaving you in charge of Patrol Leader Hislan. He will be able to make you enjoy yourselves and do some good work, I'm sure. Saye, Wards and one Tenderfoot—Law, of the Widgeons, I think—will accompany me on a small expedition. We shall not be long and I hope will give you a welcome surprise on our return. It will be up to you all to see that we don't get back without your spotting us! Troop! Dismiss!"

Keenly expectant the lads watched their three fellow Scouts march off with their S.M. Contrary to their expectations, Mr. Wayte did not use his car, but led his small party off on foot. No one was aware of the purpose of the expedition, but it was obvious from the Scoutmaster's demeanour that something unusual was afoot.

For close on two miles Mr. Wayte led his companions down the river bank, chatting to them on any matter save the business on hand. To a direct question from Saye he merely replied that time would show, adding that there was some hard work before them.

"Don't forget to keep your eyes open when moving around the district," he added. "Remember, it is a part of your work to make yourselves familiar with your surroundings wherever you are. I shall probably ask you one of these days to draw a plan of the vicinity of the camp, or a certain part of it, and I want a return of at least seventy-five per cent. accurate. Describe our journey so far, Law. Think carefully before you reply—I don't want you to rush it and forget any important facts."

The Tenderfoot reddened as he received the order. He had certainly kept his eyes open as he walked, but to put it all into words appalled him at first. Mr. Wayte was afraid that the lad would baulk, but he began, slowly at first, then with increasing confidence. " Leaving the camp, we walked nearly 150 yards in an easterly direction, through a copse of hazel, pine and oak trees, and plenty of undergrowth of blackberry bushes and grass," he said. " Our path was merely a track through the trees, just about six feet wide all the way. We came to a winding road, between high hedges, that ran mainly north and south and turned to the right. The road itself was of the usual type of country byway found in this part of the country and was very dusty. At irregular intervals on each side, in the hedge, oak trees were growing, while wisps of straw on the road itself and in the hedge, together with broad tracks of wheels and of a walking horse of a large size showed that a farm cart had passed along fairly recently, for the tracks were only crossed by those of a bicycle, which, judging by the marks of the tyres, was the one ridden by Bell this morning. These marks I saw near where we first came on to the road and, going by the line they took, I think Bell made a mistake and started off the wrong way at first, for the spoor made a turn in the road, crossing over the cart tracks and then went straight along the middle of them.

"After half a mile along the road we passed through a gate on the right side and crossed a large field in a south-westerly direction, striking a path by the river bank, along which we have been walking about a quarter of an hour, having climbed over two stiles and through one gate. There is wooded country all along the other bank and ahead of us and to our left. That's about all, sir."

"Very good beginning, Law, but it was rather lacking in detail towards the end," criticised Mr. Wayte. "I must confess I didn't notice those tracks of the bicycle myself, but I saw the farm cart. But, tell me, how did you know the cyclist was going the same way as the farm cart? I didn't see you stop and examine them."

"I didn't, sir," came the reply. "But

I saw that they were on each side of the road as soon as we struck it and thought at first that someone had ridden both ways, although the tracks looked about the same age somehow. But a little further on I saw the left-hand mark curve round to my right and knew that the one on the right was the last one taken, because there was the word ' Cambridge ' on the tyre of the front wheel— shown by an occasional loop—and the marks of a Dunlop Magnum on the back one. West's bike has those tyres on it, and I knew Bell had borrowed it this morning. Because the tracks on the right kept immediately in the middle of the cart's tracks, I decided that was the way the cycle was going—it was on the left side of the road going in the direction of the village."

" Very creditable, Law ; you must keep that kind of deduction up—it's a great thing. We'll pull Bell's leg about starting off the wrong way when we get back and see what he says," exclaimed the Scoutmaster. " Try and notice signs in open country, in the grass and hedges and all around as you did on the dusty road and you will do well. For instance, did you notice a grass snake just off the path about two hundred yards back, and a hedgehog a few yards back ? You didn't ? Well, they were there. Did you see them, Saye or Wards ? "

" I saw the hedgehog, sir," answered Saye. " I pointed it out to Wards. I saw the cycle and cart tracks, too, but I certainly didn't notice which way they were travelling."

" No, you were too busy trying to find out what is the object of this little jaunt," stated Mr. Wayte. " Talk as much as you like when the coast is clear, but always keep your eyes open and mind alert whatever else you are doing. It is amazing what a lot you can learn from small signs when you have the facility. That facility is gained by practice. Now, I don't want to rub it in any more, and here we are at our destination. What do you see, Wards ? " He brought the party to a stop.

" Small wood to our left, sir, twenty yards of grass-covered land between its westerly side and the river. This strip of grassland stretches right ahead to the next bend of the river, about a quarter of a mile, or less, further on. Five yards ahead of us is a small creek, twenty feet wide, running to the edge of the wood. In the creek, moored to the bank by two ropes is a boat—whaler type, I think, it's called—with oars, a mast and a sail lying along the thwarts. Just by it is a small shack, built of tarred boards, and a man, of a fisherman type, is coming along a small path from the wood, and he's waving to you, sir."

"Pretty good, Wards, but you've missed one important thing regarding the boat," replied Mr. Wayte, returning the man's salute. "Do you see what it is, Saye?"

"I think so, sir," was the answer. "On the bow is painted the Scouts' emblem, and just beneath I can see the top of some letters, but the bank just cuts them off and I can't read them."

"That's what I was getting at," exclaimed the Scoutmaster. "And if you could read the inscription under the badge you would see the words '28th Portlip Troop.' That whaler—she's an ex-naval boat—is my present to the troop. I got hold of her some months ago quite cheaply and got Bran—he's the man you see over there—to have her painted up and overhauled ready for us to have her to-day. He's made a good job of it, too.

Get aboard while I have a few words with him and get her ready to take back to the camp. Go carefully, mind."

Without waiting for a second bidding, the three Scouts clambered aboard their new boat and began casting off the ropes, leaving only the bow end fast with a light slip line until Mr. Wayte joined them. The whaler was 35 feet long with rowlocks for eight oars, pointed both ends and, they found, very easy to move, although she was extremely "stiff," showing no tendency to capsize even when they were all standing on the same side—in fact she barely heeled to their weight. As Wards had stated, she was fully equipped with mast, sail, oars, boat-hooks and rudder, and there was a substantial centre-board that gave an indication that she would be handy under canvas.

Working with a will, the three lads had the mast stepped and shrouds made fast and were taking the canvas cover from the sail before the Scoutmaster stepped aboard.

"Well, what do you think of her?" he asked.

"She's gorgeous, sir!" came the response. "We don't know how to thank you for her!"

"Never mind about that. So long as you are pleased and the rest of the troop equally so, I'm satisfied. Now we must work her back to camp. I see you are getting the sail ready. We might be able to do it, but it will be close-hauled sailing most of the way and there's an ebb tide coming down already. Don't forget we don't know how she will head up to the wind yet."

"We can keep the oars handy, sir," pointed out Saye. "If she is slow in coming round we can help her with them."

"We can," admitted Mr. Wayte. "But that is a practice that must be avoided except in most extreme cases—it is not considered the thing, and no smart crew would dream of doing it. Sail alone or oars alone is the thing. However, there's a pretty good breeze; we'll try the canvas once we get clear of this creek. You've got the positions of the halliards all worked out, I hope? That is most important in case you have to let go in a hurry. You have? Right! Then we'll get going. Ship the rudder, cast off for'ard! That's the way! Now pole her gently astern; there's no room to use your oars properly here."

The whaler slipped easily astern as Wards plied an oar, polewise, over the bow, and under the influence of the rudder, controlled by the Scoutmaster, described a curve when she entered the river proper and lay with her bows pointing up stream. The three Scouts were no novices in the art of boat handling—they had all done a certain amount in Portlip harbour from time to time—and, in obedience to an order, quickly lowered the centre-board, ran up the standing lug-sail, made fast the tack and passed the main sheet to Mr. Wayte in the stern. Then, as the boat gathered way, they hoisted the jib, and sheeted it home on the lee side. Five minutes after receiving the order to hoist sail the work was done, and the three Scouts were sitting quietly to windward, while the craft slipped silently and easily through the water, ready for the next command.

Nursing the helm carefully, the Scoutmaster took every advantage of the puffs of the breeze as the boat sailed close into the wind. He hoped to reach the next bend in the river without making a " tack " and, to his delight, found that the craft headed up well and made little or no leeway. With ample water to leeward, he cleared the point that had at first caused his doubt, and gently put the tiller up and eased off the main sheet as the wind was brought more on the port beam. As he sailed the whaler, he carefully explained all the points of the art to his youthful crew, although they followed his moves easily from their own experiences.

"She seems to handle very well in a light breeze," he stated, as he relaxed somewhat. "She should do the same in a stiff blow, but we shall have to try it before we are sure. You all saw how I 'weathered' that point by 'luffing' slightly at each puff, didn't you? At each puff of wind I gently put the helm down until the sail was nearly shaking, then put it up again to get way once more. By this means I made the boat shoot slightly to windward each time and gained a yard or so in that direction, and managed to clear the mud on the lee side without making a tack. I'm afraid it's easier to do than describe, but you all saw me perform the trick —I hope you'll bear it in mind when you are in charge of the helm under sail. Later on I will give you all instruction in doing it yourselves, but now we have to get back to the camp as soon as we can—the others are equally entitled to having their share. Only another quarter of a mile to do before we reach Bos'n's Wharf. We've come along well."

They had; the journey that had taken them close on an hour ashore had been practically covered in half that time on the water, but it was a slightly shorter distance. Slightly on the starboard side bow they could see the tents and slight smoke from the camp fire, but there was no sign of the Scouts in the vicinity.

" I believe we shall get in without them seeing us in spite of your warning, sir ! " exclaimed Saye, chuckling at the thoughts of the troop's surprise when they found the boat in the dock by the camp. " We'll have caught them properly this time."

" We'll see," responded Mr. Wayte. He had learned to anticipate the unexpected, and had great faith in his Scouts. " Hislan is not often caught napping, and he did have some sort of warning, at least."

But as they drew near the camp, he began to have his doubts. The place seemed as silent as a grave. Twenty yards from the dock he gave the order to down sail and up centre-board and, when the command had been carried out, told his crew to out oars and pull alongside.

Barely had Saye obtained a hold on the side of the dock with a boat-hook when, to the accompaniment of the Troop Call, the remaining Scouts leapt up from their places of concealment in the vicinity and ran cheering to greet the four adventurers.

CHAPTER VI

THE TROOP WHALER

"WELL done; you've caught us that time!" exclaimed Mr. Wayte, as the calls died down. "We anticipated surprising you and failed!"

"It was just a stroke of luck, sir," acknowledged Hislan. "It just happened that I was out in the clear space over there some minutes ago, watching for the others through my field glasses. They were converging on me under cover and I was out to catch them before they got to within ten yards of me. By chance, I looked down the river at the bend and saw the nose of the boat come round. The next thing I noticed was the Scouts' emblem on the bow, although I was not too sure about that, but directly I caught sight of the four of you I guessed who it was. The glasses are jolly good and I was soon certain, so I called the others up, gave them the word of your arrival, and we staged the little affair. I'm glad we surprised you, at any rate, sir."

" I don't think you did quite," objected Saye. " Mr. Wayte was not too sure that we would be able to come up unnoticed, although we couldn't see anyone about. When I remarked that we had you all cold, he just said ' We'll see,' and he was right ! "

The Scoutmaster smiled. " I did have an idea that you were planning something," he admitted. " Bearing in mind that I have warned you all not to get too far away from the camp and leave it unguarded in case of unlawful visitors. I thought it strange that no one at all was visible. All the same, your reception was a surprise, and a treat, too. Now, tell me, what do you think of the troop's latest acquisition ? " he added, indicating the whaler.

" A present from Mr. Wayte himself ! " shouted Saye. " Three cheers for Mr. Wayte ! "

The Scouts responded heartily and crowded round the edge of the dock to thank their S.M. and examine the boat. For fully ten minutes the four voyagers were busy answering all manner of questions until the Scoutmaster checked the flow and, looking at his watch, which showed 1 p.m., ordered the Scouts to dinner. " Food first—I hope the cooks for the day have done their job properly, for I'm positively starving," he stated. " Then rest—you all know the routine—and then perhaps we shall have some boating, although the tide is on the ebb. Moor the whaler at the entrance of the dock so that she will have plenty of water, Saye and Wards ; then leave her alone until we are ready to use her. The rest get ready for dinner."

Tearing themselves away from the boat with an effort, the lads obeyed orders. The craft was the beginning of a long-promised course Mr. Wayte had outlined to them ; it was hardly a surprise, for he had said they should have one as soon as possible, but none had even dreamed that it would be theirs so quickly. Mr. Wayte had suggested to them that the troop should be formed into a Marine section—a combination of Land and Sea Scouts—and they had enthusiastically welcomed the plan. At first, the idea had been to change them over to Sea Scouts proper, but they all wanted to continue with the usual Scout work ashore, much as they hankered after the other. Their Scoutmaster's suggestion had settled the problem without difficulty; in fact they marvelled that there was not an official section of " Marines," as they voted to designate themselves.

The savoury stew dished up from the steaming mess tins soon made them forget their excitement for some minutes as they became aware of their hunger and they were soon busy disposing of their food, although they had one topic of conversation only during the meal—the boat.

Directly the plates were empty they all turned to, to wash and clear up ; then Mr. Wayte told them to fall in.

" In five minutes—one-thirty, to be precise— you all have to have one hour's rest," he stated. " During that time there is to be no. talking or moving about. Anyone not conforming to these orders will not be allowed to go in the whaler this afternoon. At two-thirty I will begin to give you some instruction in boat-handling, and give you some practice in rowing. When you have success-fully mastered the control of the boat under oars, you will learn to handle her under sail, so it's up to you all to do your best to get

the first part over quickly. I am hoping
that you will be sufficiently proficient by the
time we strike camp to sail her back to Portlip with most of the gear aboard. Bear that
in mind—it will save some of you a long
march—and remember there's to be no fooling
about while you are afloat. I maintain you
are one of the smartest troops in Portlip
ashore; see that you fill the same place afloat
when you have obtained proficiency on the
water. Now dismiss. Each Scout may choose
his own resting place, but beware of lying
about unprotected in the sun. Carry on!"

After strolling over to see that the whaler
was riding nicely to her ropes and properly
secured, the Scoutmaster retired to the privacy
of his own tent and produced a well-seasoned
briar, filled it, lit it, and sat back contentedly
drawing at his old friend while he read the
newspaper that Bell had brought him that
morning. He made it a strict rule never to
smoke in the presence of his Scouts and looked
forward to his hour's seclusion that the com-
pulsory rest order brought him. But he
candidly admitted to his friends that the
thus enforced cutting down of smoking did
him a world of good and the few pipes he

had when away from the troop were quite worth waiting for—he enjoyed them more than when he was smoking in his usual heavy way.

Reading quietly in the cool of his tent, he found the time pass quickly. There was not a sound from outside to indicate the presence of eighteen Scouts, but the lads themselves, obeying orders to the word, thought the sixty minutes of silence would never pass. Time and time again they consulted their watches or watched the changing shadows thrown by the sun, but at length they heard the welcome sound of the Scoutmaster's whistle calling them to fall in.

" Patrol leaders. March your patrols to the boat ! " ordered Mr. Wayte. Then, when they were in position, he instructed the leaders to get aboard and pass out the masts and sails.

" Step on board, one at a time," was the next command. " Mind you don't all get on one side ; she's safe enough, but that's a rule you must never forget. Spread yourselves out and sit down, but keep away from the stern sheets—that's my place. Now," he resumed, as he entered the well-laden boat

himself, " we'll just run over the various
names of the different parts for a start, until
you all know them perfectly. No one must
forget any of these names, for it might be
necessary for me to order one of you to do
something in a hurry and it would perhaps
be fatal if the Scout named didn't know
what I was referring to. Now we'll begin."

For close on half an hour Mr. Wayte pointed
out the various portions of the craft with
their allotted nautical terms, how to boat
an oar, step the mast, toss oars, lay on oars,
coil, throw, and make fast the painter, and
the hundred and one other things that crop
up in the handling of a boat. Then, knowing
full well the folly of overdoing a thing, he
ordered the Widgeons to go ashore and watch
while the Bulls rowed the whaler up and
down a short stretch of the river.

For the most part the lads could handle
an oar, but they found the heavy ash ones
were quite a different matter to the light
ones used in ordinary pleasure boats on
a river and at the seaside, but with very few
spills in the form of " catching crabs " they
soon got into a fairly good swing and found
that the comparatively big craft was sur-

prisingly light to row. All too soon for them, but none too soon for the Widgeons; the Scoutmaster ordered them to get ashore and give the other patrol a chance to show what they could do.

Rapidly the change of crews was effected and once more the whaler moved up and down the stretch of river opposite the camp, haltingly at first and then with increasing smoothness as the Widgeons found their stroke and accustomed themselves to the heavy oars. Then, the allotted time expiring, she was brought alongside and the troop formed up ashore.

" Not bad for a first attempt," stated Mr. Wayte. " In a very short time I can see you all pulling together well; you are somewhat ragged and inclined to ' windmill ' at present. Remember, all of you, that it is only necessary to lift the blade of the oar, at the end of the stroke, just clear of the water. A twist of the wrist will turn the flat of the oar so that it will skim over the water if a wave happens to strike it—there is no need to lift it a foot or more as you did to-day. Not only is it a waste of energy, but it looks bad. A well-trained and efficient

D*

crew will handle the oars as one and get more out of their work than when the oars are moving like flails.

"Now I am going to pick a crew from the two patrols. The best oarsmen will stay ashore and begin to prepare tea while I give the others some coaching in rowing. Saye, Raine, Bell, Hislan, Wards, Smith, Oaks and Elson will fall out for domestic work; the others, get aboard. Eight at the oars and the remaining two as bowmen and stern sheets man respectively. You two will attend to the painters and boat-hooks when necessary. All aboard? Right. Cast off! Push off for'ard! Push off aft! The remainder, toss oars!"

The unaccustomed orders were carried out with a semblance of smartness, but the oarsmen found their part somewhat of a strain for want of practice. The heavy ash oars had to be lifted from their resting places over the thwarts and hoisted up until the blades were poised at right angles to the keel of the boat and the hafts resting on the bottom boards.

"Now shove her astern, bowman. That's right; gently does it!" ordered the S.M.

Then as the boat drifted clear of the dock, he gave the command for the rowers to drop their oars and pull easily ahead.

With a series of splashes the oars fell into the rowlocks and the lads went through the motions of rowing with little success. In the first stroke two " crabs " were caught by the youngest members of the crew and three more blades fouled each other.

" That won't do ! " shouted Mr. Wayte. " A disgraceful display. Toss oars again. Now, when I give the order ' Give 'way' again, drop your oars together, taking your time from the stroke. Then as he makes his first pull, do you all likewise at the same time and speed. Try again. Give 'way ! "

This time it was better. True, there were some slow ones, but the Scoutmaster realised that it is not an easy task to perform the motions neatly without much practice, and that his crew was composed of fairly young boys, and was satisfied. After twenty minutes, hard striving the whaler was moving over the water at a fair rate of speed with few casualties in the way of " crabs." Then he directed that the boat should be returned to her mooring-place.

" Now we will make her fast for the night,"
he decided, as they ran alongside the dock.
" Two of you stay aboard for a few minutes.
One of you take this rope to the far side of
the dock and throw an end to the bowman.
You do the same with this one, only heave
it to the man aft," he directed.

Under his commands this was carried out,
and ten minutes later the whaler was secured
in the centre of the waterway between four ropes
—two ahead and two astern—that stretched
from her to opposite sides of the dock.

" She'll be safe now as the tide rises and
falls," he pointed out. " Furthermore, she
will be afloat all the time and we shall be able
to get at her at any moment we want her,
slacking off those far ropes and hauling in
those on this side. Now for tea ! Come on ! "

" Aren't we going out in her any more
to-day ? " asked Saye anxiously, as Mr. Wayte
approached.

" Not to-day," came the reply. " You've
had quite enough and there's nothing like
taking it in small doses at first. I'll warrant
there'll be some sore hands by bedtime, as
it is ! "

" I've heard it mentioned already, sir ! "

acknowledged Saye. " But they all say it's worth it."

" That's the spirit ; I shouldn't like to hear any of the troop complain of hard work. What has the quartermaster dished up for tea to-day ? I'm quite ready for it, by Jove ! "

" Tea, bread, butter, marmalade or jam, and buns, sir."

" The very thing ! " exclaimed Mr. Wayte. " The local baker makes jolly good bread and if his buns are up to the same standard we shall be in luck's way. They ought to be ; we'll see ! "

The meal was excellent and the Scouts did it full justice ; but then came the less appreciated task of washing and clearing up once more. Each Scout had to clean his own knife, cup and plate and the camp orderlies for the day attended to the billies in addition. Within a few minutes the task was completed—many hands making light work of it—and the Scoutmaster ordered the expectant lads to fall in.

" To a certain extent we have departed from our mapped-out routine to-day," he began. " I anticipated that when I planned to bring the boat up this morning. It is not a serious matter—we are all here to enjoy ourselves and the routine chart was merely to keep us from wasting time in debating 'What shall we do now?' However, there is one thing we have left undone, I notice, and it can easily form a part of this evening's programme—recreation and camp games. The patrols have not yet made their totem poles, and there have been one or two items to-day that deserve a notch, I think. Very well, you have one hour in which to make these totems —one for each patrol—and you have to use your own ingenuity in their construction. Patrol Leaders, carry on!"

The patrols marched off the camping ground into the wood, intent on finding suitable material for their purpose. The Scoutmaster stood watching them until they were lost to sight in the trees and then made his way to his tent where, after lighting his pipe (the second that day) he busied himself with writing letters and looking over accounts, but keeping an eye on his watch as he worked.

Long before the allotted time was up, he heard the two patrols return and set up their trophies, but he made no move, knowing that if he was wanted he would be asked for.

So long as the lads were occupied he let them carry on. Then, as the watch marked off the hour, he moved from his tent, blowing his whistle for the " fall in," adding the words, " each patrol by its totem pole."

Moving across to the Bulls, he critically inspected their work. The lads had found a gnarled oak branch that resembled the crude shape of the animal's head from which they took their name. Two pointed, slightly curving sticks had been added to serve as horns, while pieces of bark did duty for ears. The whole was set up on a stout hazel stick that was set up in the ground.

" Very creditable," he commented. " But you might have given it eyes. Fall out, light the council fire and stay until I join you."

Then he moved across to the Widgeons' tent. Their effort also represented their patrol, for a roughly carved bird—presumably a widgeon—with bark wings partially out-stretched as if in the act of " taking off " surmounted their pole, and for some moments Mr. Wayte was at a loss to decide on which was the better of the two. Then he ordered the Bird section over to the council fire, which was just beginning to burn up.

Instructing the troop to squat, he seated himself on a log and addressed the circle.

" Your totems are extremely good in both cases," he began. " I have not yet decided which patrol shall gain the notch for having made the better one ; we will leave it for the time being. You all know that any good work by a patrol is rewarded by one notch. Individual notches are given to any member of a patrol, but these only count as one sixth of a patrol one. That is the usual ruling. Now, we can begin on the small notches, which we will term ' nicks.'

" The first nick, I think, should be awarded to P.L. Saye for his brake on the trek cart. Another goes to Bell for bringing me back a morning paper when he fetched the mails. Hislan gets one for his work in looking after the camp this morning and spotting us in the whaler on our return, and one goes to Tender-foot Law for a smart piece of observation on the road this morning. Before I tell you what it was, I want to ask Bell one question. It is this : Why did you take the wrong direction when you started out for the village this morning ? "

The troop secretary blushed slightly. " I

did not make a mistake, sir," he reported. "I came along the path to the road faster than I should have done, and as I cleared the trees at the edge, I saw the road was practically blocked by a farm cart loaded with straw. Instead of putting on my brakes, I slewed round to the right behind the cart, cycled a few yards along the road, then turned and overtook the cart further along where it had enough room to let me pass. That's all, sir."

"I see," resumed the Scoutmaster. "You will perhaps wonder why I asked that question ; Law, when I asked him to give a description of the road we had passed along, told me, among other things, that the tracks showed that a cart, loaded with straw, had passed along, and that a cyclist, whom he identified as Bell by the marks of the tyres, started off in the wrong direction for the village, turned and followed up the cart. I did not notice this myself, and my question was just to verify his statement. You heard the answer and, I am sure, will agree it is worth one nick. That makes the two patrols equal in nicks, and I have a notch to award for the poles themselves. After due deliberation, I have decided that the efforts deserve a tie ;

you will take one notch each and start off 'all square.' Now, we have camp games on the programme. Get to it—you have barely an hour before we have our evening cocoa and biscuits. Then comes camp fire and bed."

With a cheer for their Scoutmaster, the troop fell to the joys of a good old rough and tumble. When the time came, they were all ready for bed.

CHAPTER VII

MR. "X" ARRIVES

THE following day passed busily, but quietly. More used to the routine, the Scouts found the cleaning-up tasks were quickly disposed of and time was devoted to bathing, scouting practice, boat-instruction, games and, of course, the camp fire before turning in, but, all the same, Saye and Bell found time to discuss their plan and arrange a few minor details. Mr. "X" was expected the following day, so the P.L. arranged that he should be duty officer for the time. This was rather essential, for no Scout was allowed to leave the camp without permission either from the " duty officer " or Mr. Wayte himself, and Saye did not want to have to let anyone else into the secret. Three was enough until they knew if the plan was successful or not; then, if so, the whole troop would be acquainted with the facts and work them out to their ultimate success—or failure. They had decided that Law would be the Scout for their errand and it only remained for them to " wangle " him from Hislan when the time came. It was a pity he was not in their own patrol, but, after all, it would mean that all the kudos would not be absorbed by the Widgeons alone. Furthermore, Law was a quiet lad about the camp and his absence would hardly be noticed, but he was as sharp as a needle as regards picking up signs and information, which he usually kept to himself.

" Look here, Law," remarked Saye, when he and Bell found the Tenderfoot at a quiet moment. " You know Mr. ' X ' is expected to-morrow, don't you ? Well, we have a little job for you then. I expect there will be a ' fall in ' when he turns up, and as soon as possible after I want you to come to me and I'll tell you what to do. Don't say a word to anyone else in the meantime, but for your information I'll just mention the fact that your errand will be to help us identify Mr. ' X ' and find out his real name and address. We are keeping the plan to ourselves until we find out whether it works or not, then, if we are successful, we shall tell the Troop. But don't think we shall get to know all we want to to-morrow—it will probably take some time. Right you are, buzz off now ! "

There was an undercurrent of excitement in the camp from réveillé onwards. All hands knew of the possibility of Mr. " X's " arrival and arrangements made. The whole camp and every bit of equipment was cleaned up, and the Scouts themselves saw that they were as smart as if they were in their own hall, but for the fact that they had discarded their stockings and wore only plimsolls on their feet—obeying the standing camp order of " proper Scout dress to the knees."

Acting on the assumption that the visitor could hardly be expected to put in an appearance during the forenoon—owing to the remoteness of the camp—Mr. Wayte carried out the boat practice before lunch instead of after, as usual. The patrol remaining ashore posted sentries at the coppice entrance near the road, to give the alarm if Mr. " X " turned up, but the whole time passed without interruption.

" Hello, what are you at, Saye ? " asked Mr. Wayte, as he brought the Bulls ashore just before the midday meal, glancing at the Widgeons' Leader, who was seated on the ground, busy with a fine strip of leather.

" Making up a ' woggle,' sir," came the reply, as the Scout rapidly threaded an end through seemingly intricate curves. " I've just one finished and thought perhaps Mr. ' X ' might like it as a kind of souvenir. I know he doesn't wear a scarf, but I can't think of anything else just now."

" Slightly small for a woggle, I should say," commented the S.M. critically. " What are you using to make it ? "

" A leather bootlace I had in my kit, sir," Saye answered the question first. " As regards size, I've made it so that it will just about fit an average walking stick. I think it should look pretty good just below the handle, and I know Mr. ' X ' used one. That's finished it ; he can come as soon as he likes now," concluded the Senior P.L., deftly securing the ends. He had a reason for choosing the particular type of present. Made like an open " Turk's head," the emblem would be a unique and distinctive mark on their bene-factor's stick which (if its owner fixed the adornment as he proposed to suggest) would

be readily picked out by the keen-eyed troop
directly they spotted it. He was doing his
best to lay a trail.

" He'll be glad to know you've all thought
of him, at any rate," acknowledged Mr. Wayte.
" We must try and get him to stay the night
in camp; there's room in my tent. By the
way, as you are so good at those things, you
might put a couple on the whaler's tiller—it
will smarten it up a lot. Hello, they're ready
with the grub; we'd better hurry and not
waste time. I hope there's plenty of grub
well cooked in case he turns up in time to join
our festive board."

The meal was finished and all signs of it
cleared away, but still the troop waited for
Mr. " X." Hislan, during dinner, suggested
that an outpost on a cycle should be posted
along the road during the afternoon to give
a warning of their visitor's approach. " It
would be jolly good to let him come into
a deserted camp and, while he was wondering
what was the matter, we could all rush in
from all sides," he exclaimed.

" It would be a welcome," admitted Mr.
Wayte, " but the cyclist might be spotted
and that would give the show away. It's

a good chance of some scouting practice, though. One Scout could go down the road, hide himself from anyone approaching from Redley, yet remaining in sight of a second Scout posted nearer camp and signal directly he saw Mr. 'X' coming along. The second sentry would pass the word on to a third, and so on until the news reached the main body. Then the outposts would have to get back as quickly as possible, without being seen, to take up their ' welcome positions.' How will that do ? "

" Fine, sir ! " came a chorus of approval. " Can we start now ? "

" One hour's rest as usual first," insisted the Scoutmaster firmly. " After that you can all carry on. If Mr. 'X' turns up during the rest, we must put up with it ! "

Mr. Wayte had no trouble in enforcing the sixty minutes' silence and rest, but there were obvious signs of unrest and impatience throughout the troop while it lasted. Lying on the ground in various positions, every one of the eighteen Scouts raised his head from time to time and peered anxiously along the path leading to the road and shifted several times as the irksome minutes passed, but at long length the S.M's. whistle broke the spell and they eagerly fell in to decide on the pickets.

Two Scouts from each patrol were chosen for the work and sent off to take up advantageous positions. Before they left, Mr. Wayte impressed on them the importance of keeping within view of each other, yet out of sight of anyone on the road, and of getting back to camp silently and quickly. " Remember, if you are seen the whole scheme will fall flat," he warned them. " If you are a long time getting back you will miss the first part of the fun. The three inner pickets must keep a sharp look-out for signals from the outpost and pass them on at once. I suggest you just wave a white handkerchief when you are sure your quarry is coming along; three flicks will mean ' Stand by.' This should be given when the outpost sights someone and can't pick him out for sure. Using one and three waves as signals should not lead to any confusion. Now, get off sharp ! "

As soon as the small party disappeared, the Scoutmaster rehearsed the remainder in their part. Each lad found a place of concealment on the edge of the clearing, hid himself and, on a signal from the S.M. (a sharp, low blast on his whistle) the whole troop sprang from its hiding places and rushed to the centre of the camp cheering as it ran.

" Good ! " exclaimed the Scoutmaster. " Do the same when the time comes and you'll bring it off well. Not a sound, mind, while you are waiting for the signal. Break off now and amuse yourselves as you please, but be ready to take up your position on the first order from me. Keep within the camp and enjoy yourselves. Remember Mr. ' X ' may not turn up after all."

The lads moved off in small groups talking hard. Some busied themselves in making the camp even more spick and span—if that were possible—while others stood looking at their boat and naming all the parts Mr. Wayte had taught them in her construction and gear. But it was easy to see that they were all on the alert for the big happening of the day—if it came off.

Precisely at 3.15 (three-quarters of an hour after " turn to " time following the rest) the inner picket came running up and panted out that the signal had been passed back.

"Roughly ten minutes' wait, I should say," observed Mr. Wayte, when he had ordered the troop to fall in. "Mr. 'X' should be three-quarters of a mile off by road and track, but considerably less as the crow flies so we must keep quite quiet and take up our positions. Settle yourselves comfortably in your places, keep your heads down and don't move about. Bear in mind that we do not know how much Mr. 'X' knows of woodcraft, so we must not make the mistake of under-rating his powers. This means you must all take the greatest care not to raise suspicion, or the whole affair will fall flat. Listen for my signal and act directly you hear it."

Swiftly the Scouts took up their stations, the Scoutmaster remaining in the centre of the ground while they took cover, naming any of the troop he could see when they were settled and making him conceal himself better.

Within a short while he was satisfied and silently took up his own position waiting, like all the Scouts, excited in anticipation of their visitor's surprise.

So well did the troop take cover and remain quiet that before the thuds of Mr. " X's " footsteps (plainly audible to the S.M., who had one ear pressed to the ground) became loud, the birds had resumed their twittering in the trees around them, only to fly away at the sounds of the rapidly approaching steps.

Peering cautiously through a screen of bracken that was in front of him, the Scout-master saw the well-remembered form of the troop's benefactor stride vigorously into the clearing, with his sheepdog at his heels. For a few seconds Mr. ' X ' gazed intently round, as if surprised at the stillness. Then a slight smile played round his mouth ; he had a trump card and was going to use it.

" Find 'em, Nan ! " he commanded, addressing the dog.

Like an arrow from a bow the huge animal bounded across the cleared space towards the trees. There was no doubt that the dog had sensed the presence of the Scouts, for she darted straight " up wind " towards the strongest scent. This was a move that

Mr. Wayte had not foreseen and bid fair to disorganise seriously the whole scheme. The Scouts could not be expected to carry out their part in the face of a charging $4\frac{1}{2}$ stone of dog.

Before Nan was half-way across the open space the whistle trilled. Like magic a ring of Scouts rose and ran, as rehearsed, towards their visitor, but there was a gap on the threatened sector and evidently agitated shrubs showed that someone was in full retreat through the copse in that direction.

A sharp, peremptory shout of " Nan ! " cut through the roar of cheers from at least fifteen throats. In spite of the confused noise, the sheepdog heard her master's order, pulled up short and trotted obediently back to her owner's feet, ignoring the ring of Scouts entirely.

" Thank you all ; that was a right royal welcome—I'm sorry I messed up a bit of it ! " exclaimed Mr. " X " speaking to all members of the troop as he shook Mr. Wayte by the hand. " I can tell you I was a bit taken aback to find a deserted camp— although there's no reason why it shouldn't be at this time of the day, I'm sure. But there was one thing that made me a trifle suspicious—I was certain you would not have left the camp with the tent doors wide open, even in this secluded spot. Accordingly, I took a chance with Nan. There is little that escapes her and I knew she would not harm anyone, however fierce her looks were, in the circumstances. She can hurt if necessary, but if I had let her go on she would have merely rounded you all up, as if you were a straggling flock of sheep, by snapping at your heels and racing round in ever-decreasing circles. Well, how are you all? Snugly settled down?"

"We are, thanks to you, Mr. 'X'" replied the Scoutmaster. "We have every bit of the gear we originally intended to get and it is all open to your inspection."

"Don't think I have come here to poke and pry," objected the visitor. "I really wanted to see how you were and get better acquainted."

"Good! Then you can stay with us for a bit?" asked Mr. Wayte. "The troop has been looking forward to your visit and hopes you will give me the pleasure of sharing the tent that the Scouts presented me with.

There's plenty of room, and we have a spare blanket or two. They'll be very disappointed if you don't."

" By Jove ! I'd like to ! " came the reply. " I meant to put up at the village inn, as a matter of fact, but you look so comfy here that I'll forego the local hostel with pleasure. I'll get my bag later on."

" Let one of the lads save you the journey," suggested the S.M. " One would be pleased to go."

" Thanks, but I'll get it myself—you forget that I want to save fifty pounds by keeping my name from you ! " was the laughing response. " I'm not going to make it easy for you, you know ! "

Mr. Wayte smiled in reply. The troop was going to have a big job with the mysterious Mr. " X " he reflected. " As you like," he agreed. " But will you inspect the troop, tents and gear ? They expect it. By patrols, near your tents, fall in ! " he shouted.

Smartly the Scouts obeyed, and, accompanied by the Scoutmaster, Mr. " X " gravely looked at each lad, the tents and gear as requested, showing by his manner that it was not the first time he had attempted such a task.

" Fine crowd ! " was his comment when he had finished. " A model camp ; best I've seen for years, but I didn't expect anything else from you. I can only say I am not at all disappointed. Now, carry on with your usual routine ; don't let me interrupt in any way and give me the tip where I can join in and make myself useful."

" They've done pretty well," admitted the S.M. " Especially when you remember this is their first actual camp. I kept them hard at the theory right from the beginning and I'm glad to say they have remembered it all well. Until tea-time they have scouting games in the neighbourhood, but as there is not much time left they will stay in the camp itself. Perhaps you would like to have a pipe in my tent while they get going ? I make it a rule not to smoke in their presence myself."

Mr. " X " agreed and after the S.M. had dismissed the troop to its games, he accompanied Mr. Wayte to his tent to smoke and, as he expressed it, " to get better acquainted." Within ten minutes games were in full swing and no one noticed Saye and Bell give Law his final instructions and send him off quietly on a bicycle towards Redley, nor was his absence noticed.

Speeding along to the village, the Tenderfoot dismounted from his cycle and carefully examined every motor car that he saw in the road and in the one garage Redley boasted of. He had to get to work cautiously, for he did not want to attract more attention than was necessary. The three cars standing in the main street were easy enough. Dawdling past, he noted the numbers and general appearance and quickly came to the conclusion that none of them was owned by Mr. "X." Two were smart saloon cars and one a three-wheeler. The first was ruled out when its owner came from the local shop, got in and drove away. The second was obviously a lady's car, judging by the vase of flowers and feminine coat lying over the back of the driver's seat, and the three-wheeler contained a crate of eggs perched on the spare seat and another on the floor.

Mr. "X" was hardly the type of man to drive about with eggs, Law reflected, and,

E

furthermore, there would have been no room for the dog as well as the driver in the vehicle.

The local garage was a different matter. It was situated at the back of the one hotel of the village and approachable only through the wide gates of the stable yard. For a few minutes the Scout thought furiously. He must find some excuse to get inside and see what motors it housed. It would not do if he just walked in and nosed around ; it might lead to awkward questions.

He retraced his steps slowly down the road cudgelling his brains, staring intently at a small patch of oil, left by some car as it had stood for a while, as he passed it. The very thing ! He'd have to take a chance with his hat, but it might be worth it in the end.

Turning again he stopped with the puddle of oil directly behind him, then pushed back his hat as if mopping his forehead with his handkerchief. A slight flick with his finger and the headgear fell to the ground, just touching the oil. He had gauged it nicely.

Retrieving his fallen property with a

well-assumed expression of disgust as he saw
the black patch on its khaki brim, he looked
round as if to find some means of cleaning
off the mark, his face lighting up as his gaze
fell on the garage. The next minute he
placed his cycle by the doorpost and walked
boldly in.

" I say, could you let me have a small
drop of petrol to clean this oil off, please ? "
he asked the man in overalls who was
apparently in charge of the place. " My
hat fell off in a patch of it just over
there."

" Certainly," came the answer, and the
man moved across to a row of petrol tins
at the back of the garage. " You from the
Troop out at Bos'n's Wharf ? My mother, who
keeps the general store, told me some Scouts
were over there and doing good business
with her in the shop. Let me have your
hat ; I'll soon clean that stuff off."

Chatting to the man, the Tenderfoot moved
round the two cars that were housed in the
garage, glancing over them inside and out.
One he ruled out at once ; it was a station
'bus attached to the hotel, but the other
—a dark blue four-seater—seemed more

promising. A closer investigation showed a number of grey and black hairs on the upholstery. He was on the right track !

CHAPTER VIII

THE FIRE

"I THINK you'll find this all right," interrupted the voice of the garage hand. "A little bit stained where the petrol has cleaned up the stuff, but the oil's all out, at any rate. Lucky you brought it quick, before it soaked in."

Law took the hat with a word of thanks. He was very pleased with the way things had turned out and the mark would soon wear out, he reflected. After all, what was a small stain in his hat when £50 was at stake?

"How much do I owe you for doing that?" he asked, putting his hand in his pocket. "You've made a good job of it."

"That's all right," was the gruff reply. "I'm only too pleased to help Ma's customers in little things like that and I only drained a tin that was supposed to be empty to get

the ' juice,' so it didn't cost me anything
—you're welcome."

Bidding the man good afternoon, the
Tenderfoot left the garage, giving a second
glance at the car's number plate as he went
and reassuring himself he had committed it
properly to his memory. Yes, ZZ 99016 was
correct. He paused outside to jot the letters
and figures down in his notebook, then
climbed on his cycle and peddled as quickly
as he could back to camp. His absence
had passed unnoticed and he was able to
join the other Scouts without being seen.
The Scoutmaster and Mr. " X " were still
in the former's tent.

He was quickly joined by Saye and
Bell.

" Any luck ? " asked the P.L.

" Yes, I spotted a car in the garage—
ZZ 99016 is the number—and saw some of
Nan's hairs in the seat next to the driver's.
There was a light brown leather case in the
back, too, so I think it must be Mr. ' X's.'
' ZZ ' is the Sandshire index letters, I believe,
and Sandshire is just outside the fifty miles
he mentioned, when he said he didn't live
in Portlip. I don't think I've made any

mistake in picking it out as his car—after all, there aren't many cars in Redley."

" Good for you, Law," exclaimed Beh. " Now you see what we have to do ? Just write to the A.A. people and ask them who is the owner of the car and there we are! Simple, isn't it ? "

" I thought that was the idea," admitted the Tenderfoot. " I noticed, too, the car had an A.A. badge on it."

" Better and better ! " applauded Saye. " Carry on like this and you'll be a tip-top Scout by the time you're finished ! I'll write that letter to-morrow and, with luck, we'll have a reply before we leave here. There's no time now and the last post will have left before we will be able to post to-night."

Soon after tea was finished, Mr " X " was shown the whaler by the proud troop. He examined her critically from stem to stern, and gravely congratulated them on possessing her. " You've got a stout craft there, all right," he stated. " Did she come out of the camping fund, too ? "

" No, sir," replied Saye. " Mr. Wayte gave her to us the day after we got here and he had been giving us instructions in handling her since then."

"Very good thing too!" asserted Mr. "X." "Nothing like it. Can you handle her under sail yet?"

"We've only used the oars so far, sir," answered Hislan. "Although we all come from a sea town, only a few of us know anything about boats. But we are all going hard at it to get proficient. Mr. Wayte has promised to show us sailing to-morrow."

"Excellent! I must beg or steal a place in her crew, then. There's nothing I like more than a good sailing craft and a smart crew. Now I'm afraid I must go and get my bag, as I am going to put up here for the night."

"Only for the night, sir?" asked Saye. "We hoped you would stay some time."

"Much as I'd like to, I can't manage it just now, I'm afraid. However, I'll see if I can come along again before you break camp. Now I must find Mr. Wayte and tell him I'm going to get my gear. No, thanks, I must get it myself. You see, it is necessary to give my real name to get possession of it —Mr. 'X' won't do!"

" Let me run you along in my car,"
suggested the S.M., when Mr. " X " told him
of his intention. " I promise I won't pass
any information on to the lads—if I find out
anything ! "

" Thanks. It would save me a long walk.
I was going to beg the loan of one of those
cycles, although it is years since I mounted
one. I like walking, but to the station and
back is rather more than I care to tackle
this evening ! "

Saye and Bell, who had overheard the
conversation, exchanged glances. So their
scheme seemed to be wiped out as useless
before it was properly started. Mr. " X "
would hardly stop at the station to deposit
his bag if he had come by car. But perhaps
it was a " blind." They'd carry on with
it, they decided, and trust to luck. In the
meantime, they pushed the Scoutmaster's car
out of its leafy shelter.

Three-quarters of an hour later the car
returned with the two men. That was nail
number two in the coffin of the plan—it
did not take that amount of time to go to the
village alone, but would just about work out
for a run to the station. Nail number three

E*

appeared when Mr. " X " lifted a dark leather suitcase from the vehicle and placed it in the tent. Law had seen one of a light hue in the other suspected car.

" Yes, I missed my 'bus," remarked Mr. " X," as he watched the S.M's. motor being stowed away in its temporary garage. " At the end of last week the transmission gave out and they say the new parts won't be down from the maker's until to-day or to-morrow. Still, I couldn't very well bring it here ; you young fellows would have too easy a job if I did. This registration business soon gives a man away ! "

So nail number four was driven home.

" Rather a coincidence your seeing that friend of yours in the village," remarked Mr. Wayte. " There seems very little here to bring people to the place."

" Yes, it was strange," admitted Mr. " X." Saye and Bell pricked their ears—here was something, at least. " He's a gentleman farmer whose place is quite near to mine. Nan was one of his dog's pups, as a matter of fact. He goes in for the Old English type of sheep dog—won't have collies or any other sort. I admire them myself and persuaded him to let me have Nan some years ago. Since then, we have been firm friends."

So there was just a chance that Law's work during the afternoon was not quite in vain. As the two men moved away, Saye and Bell talked the matter over. Find where the gentleman farmer lived and near by would be Mr. " X's " domicile. But Sandshire was a large county; it would be no easy task if the car number failed to give them any clue.

That night's camp fire was a roaring success. Mr. " X " kept all the troop enthralled with his yarns of his experiences, at home and abroad, during the time he was in the Navy. He had retired some ten years previously—" gave some other fellow a chance to stay in when they were ' axing ' the officers," he explained. " I liked the service, but was fortunate enough to be independent of it from a financial point of view. But I'll admit there are times when I wish I was still in it. However, I manage to enjoy myself ashore, with an occasional yachting trip to help things along." Of the Great War he spoke little, merely saying that he had spent most of the time in the Mediterranean. "I did manage to have a look in at Jutland, though," he stated.

Contrary to the usual routine, it was well after 10 p.m. before Mr. Wayte dismissed his troop to bed. But it was an unusual night; they seldom had the chance of listening to such stirring yarns and it was a chance not to be missed. All the same, the Scouts were reluctant to go to their tents even after the half-hour's extension, but they obeyed smartly.

It was nearly midnight before the light in the Scoutmaster's tent was extinguished and the two men settled down on their camp - made mattresses. Unasked, the Widgeon patrol had constructed one for the guest during the evening, earning an unexpected notch for their totem pole, which was awarded just before the camp fire was ended, amid applause from the Bulls.

Suddenly Mr. Wayte stirred and glanced at the luminous dial of his wristwatch, which he wore day and night. 2 a.m. What had disturbed him? Then: "Mr. Wayte!" he heard his name spoken softly by the doorway.

Moving swiftly. but silently so as not to

disturb Mr. " X "—a needless precaution, for
the call had awakened his tent-companion—
he slipped outside, to find Hislan and Law
standing there. " What's wrong ? " he
demanded. " Anything the matter ? "

" There's a peculiar glow over the trees
to the north-east, sir," explained Hislan.
" Law came out of his tent just now, noticed
it and called me. I thought I'd better wake
you, sir."

" By Jove, you're right ! " exclaimed the
Scoutmaster, looking in the indicated direction.
" A fire ! Looks as if it's at that big house
along the road. Turn out all hands ; we may
be useful ! Sharp's the word ! "

Within five minutes the troop was up
and dressed in shirts, shorts and shoes, ready
for work—a smart " turn to," considering
the short notice and comparative darkness,
for which Mr. " X " complimented them
later.

" Axes, staves, buckets, rope and
blankets ! " ordered Mr. Wayte. " Get
moving ! Two of you get hold of the First
Aid box ! All ready ! Fall in, patrols !
Scouts' Pace—Forward ! "

Alternately walking and running twenty

paces at a steady five miles an hour—the official speed for the Scouts' Pace—the troop jogged along the road. The Scoutmaster restrained the lads and kept them to the stated speed, knowing that they would arrive at their objective in a fit condition at their usual and familiar step to which they had been trained.

As they neared the scene of the fire, more details were apparent. Standing back fully a hundred yards from the road, in spacious, well-hedged grounds, was a straggling Elizabethan mansion that had been admired by all members of the troop. One wing only was occupied, they knew, and the one to the north-east was open only to visitors during the week at a small charge—the Scouts had planned to view it and its treasures later— and it was the end of this portion of the house that was blazing, while two haystacks a few feet away were burning fiercely. Strangely enough, there seemed no sign of life in the vicinity despite the glare.

Racing at top speed up the drive, closely followed by the Scouts and Mr. " X," the Scoutmaster pounded on the massive oak door, while the whole troop shouted to rouse

the occupants of the south wing. A moment
later a window was thrown open and a voice
asked what was the matter. But the ruddy
glare answered the question even as it was
being asked and the householder could be
heard calling the rest of the family and
servants.

With a series of orders, Mr. Wayte sent
the Scouts to work, some to find water and
form a chain for the buckets, while half a
dozen smashed down a door in the threatened
wing with the felling-axe and dashed inside
to rescue as much of the valuable old furniture
and tapestries as they could. But before
they got going properly they were joined by
the people of the house and the servants
—a dozen in all—in hastily donned clothes.

" I've 'phoned for the Brigade from
Blurton—its the nearest," gasped the house
owner to Mr. Wayte. " But it will be the
best part of an hour before they get here, I
expect. There are two hoses and some
ladders in the stable ! "

Led by the butler and two menservants,
some of the Scouts dashed away to get the
fire appliances, which would be more useful
than the bucket chain from a pond in the

garden. Speedily they connected up the hoses and got a good stream of water flowing on to the roof and through the windows, the pressure being supplied by an old " manual," but the volume was hardly sufficient to check the flames as they devoured the dry timber of the beams and panelling. But it served to assist in the salvage work.

Working like Trojans the other party dashed into the threatened portion of the building, as close to the fire as possible, and dragged or lifted out the furnishings, ruthlessly tearing down priceless tapestries and embroideries and throwing them out of the nearest windows to helpers on the lawn. Gasping and choking in the smoke and steam produced by the water in spite of their moistened scarves which were tied lightly over their noses and mouths, they were slowly forced back by the advancing flames, but the pile of salvaged goods grew rapidly on the lawn some distance off as a result of their labours. Directed by Mr. Wayte and Mr. " X," they succeeded in saving the valuable and historic oaken refectory table that had once been the property of the luckless King Charles I, and given to a former owner of

the mansion after the Restoration by King
Charles II on his succession, in spite of its
bulk and weight. Smashing a window completely from its frame, Saye had shouted
for a ladder to be placed on the side and
the table had been slid, legs uppermost, down
the improvised slide with no more damage
than a few scratches on its highly-polished
surface.

" Keep at it ! " shouted the Scoutmaster,
as they were slowly forced back through
the rooms by the advancing flames. " You're
doing well ! We'll soon have help from the
Brigade now, but let them see what Scouts
can do ! "

He had barely spoken when a wall crashed
abruptly at the far end of the narrow room
and a large beam fell amid a shower of plaster
and a huge wave of smoke. A second later
the gloom of the room was lightened by a
tongue of flame that shot up from the debris.
Thank goodness ! The forms of the six
Scouts were all plainly visible to the S.M.
and all on their feet, but there was a dark
form lying ominously still near the end of the
fallen timber. Who was it ?

Bell saw that someone was hurt at the

same instant and bounded forward with **Mr. Wayte**. He was first there and, turning the body over, saw that it was their friend, **Mr. " X,"** and furthermore there was a nasty gash across his forehead. Obeying a word from the S.M., he took the feet, while **Mr. Wayte** lifted the shoulders, shouting to the others to carry on and take care as he did so, and they carried the unconscious form out on to the lawn, where they proceeded to render first aid in the strong flickering light that was beginning to fade with the coming of dawn.

Leaving Bell to carry out the bandaging, after ascertaining that there was no further injury, the Scoutmaster hurried back to his party. At the same time, with a vigorous clanging of bells, the motor fire-engine from Blurton dashed on the scene. In a short space of time the high-powered hoses were beating back and subduing the flames, too late to save the greater part of the wing, but in time to prevent the rest of the mansion being touched by the fire.

Half an hour later, the bulk of the furnishings having been saved by the Scouts and household retinue, Mr. Wayte ordered his troop back to camp. There was nothing more they could do; the fire was well under control and they were all pretty well done up by their strenuous work and tired from lack of sleep.

Back in the tents, there was still work to be done. Most of the Scouts had sustained burns that required treatment, but none of them was seriously hurt—thanks to their fire-drill training. They had learned to keep away from danger, yet perform useful work. The most serious case was Mr. " X," but he had recovered sufficiently to walk back and made light of his wounded head—" Looks worse than it is ! " he stated briefly.

It was nearly noon before the camp was astir again and the cooks hastened to light their fires and prepare dinner. The whole of the routine was completely thrown out of gear for that day, but the troop was content. They had had quite sufficient running about during the early hours of the morning to satisfy the most energetic of them, but all were ready that afternoon for their boat instruction.

There was a steady, but light breeze blowing and, to the lads' delight, Mr. Wayte, prompted by Mr. " X," decided to give the first lesson in sailing to the patrols. Accordingly from 2.30 to 5 p.m., the Widgeons were under canvas —tacking, reaching, running free, wearing and coming about—without straining their already aching muscles and blistered palms. While one patrol was afloat with Mr. " X " the other was being initiated into the art theoretically under Mr. Wayte on shore, then they changed about at " half-time."

After tea they carried on with their scouting games, but the Scoutmaster noted that they chose the quietest ones.   He remained talking to their guest at the door of his tent.   Mr. " X " had yielded to the Scouts' persuasion and consented to remain until the following day to give his forehead a chance of healing before travelling.

Much to the troop's disappointment, the Scoutmaster refused to permit them to re-visit the scene of the fire

" There will be people enough for the owner to worry about hanging around," he explained.   " If there was anything we could do to help it would be a different matter, but we would only be in the way. Wait until the excitement dies down, then I'm sure we shall readily get permission to have a look round."

The Scouts saw the force of his reasoning and gave up the idea for the time being, but shortly after they began their games a second visitor walked into the camp and spoke to Mr. Wayte. They had no difficulty in recognising him as the owner of the mansion and after a few seconds the S.M's. whistle chirped the "Fall in."

"Stand at ease!" ordered Mr. Wayte. "Mr. Mannaran, the owner of the house that caught fire this morning, wishes to thank you all for the work you did. He will speak for himself."

"I cannot thank you all sufficiently for what you did this morning," he stated simply. "We had all had a late night and were sound asleep when you came along and gave the alarm—we did not even notice the crackling of the flames. But for your promptness there's no doubt that the whole house would have been destroyed, not to mention the furniture and fittings that you salved for me. Very little in that line has been lost, I am glad to say, for, as you perhaps have heard, the stuff has been in my family for hundreds of years and is considered to be without price for its historical value alone. I owe the saving of that to you, and I feel that I would like to make some return. What can I do for you ? "

CHAPTER IX

THE MYSTERIOUS CASE

DEEP silence greeted Mr. Mannaran's words.

"That is rather a big question to answer at once, I'll admit," he added. " I must ask you for an answer later on, after you have talked it over. In the meantime, anything I can do for you, let me know."

"Thank you, but I am afraid this troop cannot accept anything from you for the little service it rendered you this morning," explained Mr. Wayte. "Don't think I am rude putting it like this, or that we do not appreciate your kindness, but Scouts do not accept any reward for performing any good turns—they all come in in the day's work. We were only too pleased at being able to help you and are glad our efforts were of use."

"They were, by Jove!" came the reply.

" But for you all, we might have been burned to death in our beds. But that's all nonsense about not taking a present from me. A Mannaran always pays his debts ! I want to give you all something useful, so you may as well say what you want ! "

" Nothing, thanks, Mr. Mannaran," returned the S.M. firmly. " We all enjoyed the experience ; that was sufficient reward. But if you really insist on doing something for us, let the troop visit your home when it is in working order again and see the treasures. All of us would like that."

" I'm sorry you're so determined," stated the visitor. " However, you will all be my first guests when we are in running order again, for a start. But I warn you, you will hear from me before that ! Now I must ask you to excuse me ; I have a lot to do this evening. Good night ! "

Before anything more could be said, Mr. Mannaran, with a single glance round and a wave of his hand—half-salute and half-farewell—strode from the clearing.

" That's the spirit to foster in the minds of the general public," commented Mr. " X," who had been a silent, but interested spectator.

" You all have a difficult task in refusing offered rewards for services rendered, but it pays in the long run, by Jove! News of this sort soon gets round and is extremely beneficial to the Scout Movement generally, and that, after all, is what is wanted. There are still a great number of people about who belittle Scouts, saying they play around and make general nuisances of themselves. Your work this morning and refusal of any recompense is just one more little nick cut in the foundations of these people's ideas. That is your reward, and I am sure you all look at it in this light."

" Thank you, Mr. ' X,' for putting it so well," exclaimed Mr. Wayte. " I know that the work was done with no thought of personal gain by all members of the troop. The idea you expounded of assisting in obtaining the public's goodwill towards the Movement and Mr. Mannaran's thanks are quite sufficient recompense for us! But you spoke of ' nicks.' That reminds me. I meant to leave it until camp fire to-night, but I think now will do as well. I have decided to award one nick to Law for his promptness in turning out his patrol leader when he found the fire, then each patrol will have a notch for their work at the mansion. Dismiss now and put them up ! "

Joyfully the troop broke away to add to the marks on their totem poles while Mr. " X " enquired what had caused the excitement. Mr. Wayte carefully explained and took his guest to inspect the poles themselves.

" By Jove ! I wish more and more everyday that the Scout Movement was going when I was a youngster ! " remarked Mr. " X," as he accompanied the S.M. back to his tent. " Never too late to begin, you say ? I agree, but unfortunately for me, I am a busy man and could not fit in the time. True I can find a day or two every now and then, but that's not good enough —at least, that's what I think. I'd be proud to be attached to the 28th Portlip Troop, I must say ! "

" Why not, then ? " asked the S.M. " We'd all be jolly proud to number you amongst us. You could be a sort of honorary assistant Scoutmaster, I should think, and join us when you could spare the time. You would be able to give us numberless hints in the seamanship side that we are going to take up—the whaler is the start."

" That would suit me beautifully," admitted Mr. " X ". " I'm afraid my attendances would be far from regular, though. But half a tic. We must hold to our agreement, you know ! The best thing, I think, would be to leave my appointment to the troop for twelve months, or until they find out my name and address, whichever is first. That's the idea ! The day they win the fifty pounds, or the day they pay it to me, I will join up. I shall stick to my original plan and not assist them in any way, but I hope they make my joining-up day come long before the year is up ! "

The two men gravely shook hands. " I'll tell them all about it round the fire to-night," the Scoutmaster asserted.

He did. He made the announcement just before the nightly round of yarns began. His words were received by three hearty cheers from the Scouts ; they were all genuinely pleased.

" You'll join us before the summer holidays are over, sir," promised Saye, addressing Mr. " X " as soon as the tumult subsided. " You

had better begin to get your gear as soon as
you can, so that you can ' be prepared ' for
the day ! "

" Thank you, Saye," acknowledged their
guest.   " For my sake, I hope you are right !
Let me see, holidays finish about September
the nineteenth, I believe ?   I'll make a note of
that, then, and I hope you won't let me down.
Of course, I don't know what your plans
are, but, I warn you, you have a difficult
task !   As perhaps you've already noticed,
I have even taken the precaution of putting
a new collar on Nan.   Her usual one has
my name and address engraved on it, so I
took it off just before I reached the camp
the other day."

" We know that, sir," replied Hislan, amid
a roar of laughter.   " We've all looked at
it already ! "

Much to the regret of the troop, Mr. " X "
left the following afternoon, but he promised
to do his best to rejoin them before the camp
finished.

Mr. Wayte drove him to the station, and
as the car moved out on to the road, the
passenger playfully waved an object, which
was quickly recognised as Nan's usual collar,

at the Scouts who were all assembled to give him a send-off.

" That was a straight enough challenge ! " grunted Hislan. " We'll have to turn to seriously on this business and quickly too ! "

" Quite so," assented Saye. " But we can't do anything until the camp is over, unless we tumble on something when he visits us again. I'm going to put in all the time I can until the end of the hols. once we finish here ! "

" I'm with you ! " stated Hislan at once.

" I knew you would be," returned his chum. " I'm working out a plan now, but I won't say anything about it until I've got a few details fixed up."

" I missed a chance this morning," broke in Bell, who was with them. " When I was doing up his head on that lawn, his pocket book slipped out of his coat. I could see several old letters inside, but I thought it wouldn't be sporting if I looked at them —there was a button clip on the book, keeping it shut. It was a great temptation, though."

" I'm jolly glad you didn't, Les, old son," answered Saye. " We must not take any

advantage like that, but go at it in a completely above-board way. It would have been
a different matter if one of the letters had
fallen out and you had spotted the name
and address as you picked it up. Opening
the case deliberately would have been like
pocket-picking, especially as he was unconscious. No, we must have a clean report
to put in when we reveal our work."

"That's so," agreed Hislan. "We'll do it
somehow, too!"

Short as Mr. "X's" stay had been, the
Scouts missed him after he had left, but
the time passed quickly. Boating, scouting
practice, a day's hike round the immediate
countryside, gathering fuel for the fires and
obtaining provisions from the village formed
only part of the varied programme Mr. Wayte
prepared for them and, at odd moments, Mr.
Mannaran visited the camp. He said very
little, but the troop noticed that he kept
his eyes open wide when he did come and they
wondered what was in his mind.

Two days before the break-up of the camp
the entire troop turned out to assist a nearby
farmer—whose land embraced Bos'n's Wharf
and to whom they were indebted for the use

of their camping ground—in bringing in a large part of his hay crop. Turning to at 8 a.m. they worked hard until 8 p.m. with short spells for lunch and tea. Town-bred as they all were, they thoroughly enjoyed the experience and, thanks to their training at the oars of the whaler, their hands came through without any painful and annoying blisters. That evening they trundled their hastily-fetched trek cart home laden with apples, pears, vegetables, milk and butter that the farmer's wife insisted on their accepting. They had done well, indeed, in sacrificing one day's practice in their boat and part of their routine.

The following morning's post brought a postcard that puzzled Mr. Wayte. It was a printed notice from the local railway station requesting him to call and take possession of a large case that was addressed to him. He had not ordered anything to be sent to the camp and he soon found that none of his Scouts were responsible. However, it was genuine enough, although there was a possibility that there was a mistake somewhere.

He put the postcard down and picked up

another letter. This one bore a London post-mark and the writing seemed familiar ; it was from Mr. " X " asking him if he could meet him at the railway station at 11.30 a.m., in the car, to save him the long walk to the camp. " I am availing myself of the invitation you all gave me to return to the camp," it finished up. " I hope I shall not be in the way, and that I shall be able to lend a helping hand this time.—' X.' "

The Scoutmaster was delighted at the news and lost no time in acquainting the members of the troop, which shared his enthusiasm. He also mentioned the mysterious case at the station. " I don't know what it is, but I will kill two birds with one stone, as it were, when I go to meet Mr. " X " at 11.30. In the meantime, both patrols may take the whaler and have a final practice under oars ; Saye will take charge. This afternoon we shall have to start the disagreeable business of packing up, unfortunately. Now fall in for inspection ! "

Just over an hour later, having seen the troop safely afloat, Mr. Wayte climbed into his car and drove stationwards. He knew the Scouts could be trusted in the boat and had no fears in that direction. What was worrying him was, what was the case that was waiting for him at the station and who sent it ? There was a chance that Mr. " X " was responsible, but somehow the S.M. thought not. Anyway, he reflected, as he steered his 'bus along the dusty roads, he would soon have part of his question answered, if not all.

Ten minutes before Mr. " X " was due to arrive, the Scoutmaster entered the station and produced the postcard, showing it to the porter in charge.

" This 'ere's the one, sir," stated the man, pointing to a large, oblong packing case of stout wood. " Come along 'ere yesterday morning, it did, so I sent you that there card when I went 'ome last night. It be powerful 'eavy ! "

" Thanks." The Scoutmaster bent and examined the labels. It was most certainly for him, it was addressed in typewritten letters—" Wayte, Esq., 28th Portlip Troop of Scouts, In Camp at Bos'n's Wharf, Redley," and printed on the top of the labels was the name of a well-known marine engineering firm. " Very strange," he muttered to him-

self. Then aloud, to the porter, " I suppose
I'd better shift it from here ? "

" Surely sir ! " came the reply. " But 'ow
are 'ee going to do it ? "

" I think I could stow it in the back of
the car, provided we can lift it. Do you
think we could ? "

" We'll manage 'un, sir, if you'll lend a
'and," was the confident answer. " Do 'ee
'elp me and I'll get a truck along. We'll
get it outside before the train comes."

It was done ; the case was not quite as
heavy as Mr. Wayte anticipated at first and,
with Mr. " X's " assistance, it was lodged
in the dickey of the long-suffering car.

" You've chosen a strange time to import
heavy stuff into the camp," remarked Mr.
" X," as they started off. " I thought you
were finishing to-morrow."

" So we are," responded the S.M. " But
this has turned up from somewhere. I haven't
the slightest idea who sent it, but it appears
to be for me—or the troop. Judging by
the name on the labels, I should think it is
a motor—of the marine type—but it's all
a mystery to me. I suppose you haven't
anything to do with it ? "

" Not guilty ! " came the answer. " This is not one of my crimes. How are all the lads ? "

" Tophole, thanks. We haven't had the slightest bit of trouble and, except for those burns the other day, we have not had to touch the medicine chest. Pretty good for a first camp ! "

Arriving back at the camp, the two men found the whole troop ashore to welcome Mr. " X ". There was no doubt as to his popularity, for the Scouts had voluntarily cut short their time afloat on his behalf. Then all hands assisted in opening up the mysterious case.

Mr. Wayte's guess was correct, for on removing the top planks and the packing a large size " out-board " petrol motor was revealed. There was also a stout wooden framework, complete with bolts, and a sealed envelope tied to the petrol tank.

Opening the latter, the Scoutmaster scanned the contents swiftly. " To the 28th Portlip Troop, with best wishes, in recognition of a ' good turn ' performed some time ago. It is hoped that this engine will serve them well and that the enclosed wooden fitting will enable them to use the motor without trouble on the pointed stern of their whaler. No acknowledgment is necessary," he read aloud. "Well, we seem to be in luck's way," he continued. "But we shall have to find out the name of the donor and thank him in spite of that last sentence. That will be up to you!"

"I should say he lives quite close to this camp, sir!" stated Saye quietly. "In fact it couldn't be anyone else than Mr. Mannaran, as Mr. ' X ' says he is not involved in it."

"How do you make that out, Saye?"

"Because he is the only other person that knows we have a whaler, sir," came the reply. "Also the work we put in at the fire is the only good turn we've done for months. Mr. Mannaran has been looking closely at the boat since the day he called to thank us, and we turned down his offer of a reward. The fact that that letter refers to a whaler and there is a special stern attachment for the engine makes it pretty conclusive, I think."

"I am inclined to agree with you," returned the Scoutmaster. "We have only a few hours in which to confirm this and thank him. I think we can safely accept the gift without violating any of our resolutions, and all I can say is that we are jolly lucky to have such a gift—it will solve many difficulties in Portlip harbour and outside. We'll get it shipped and try it out—all hands turn to ! Law and Oates, you go to the garage and get a couple of tins of petrol—I see there is a tin of oil supplied—and bring them back as soon as you can. The rest, with the exception of the cooks, get busy in clearing the gear out of the boat to give us plenty of working room to ship the stern piece."

It meant plenty of hard work, but by dinner-time the engine was mounted securely on the boat's stern ready for a test. To the Scouts' disappointment, Mr. Wayte ordered them to knock off and have their meal before the motor was even started up, and, despite their excitement and eagerness to return to the whaler when the food was disposed of, he enforced the usual hour's rest. " You'll have plenty of time in the future to play around with the ' out-board,' " he pointed out. " Camp routine must stand and you'll all be glad of the rest before the day is finished."

The Scoutmaster had to watch the time very carefully during that hour. He, too, was itching to test the new acquisition, but for the sake of the troop discipline he forbore to leave his tent, where he was yarning and smoking with Mr. " X " until the hour had elapsed. Then he gave the order for the troop to fall in.

" The greater number of you are going to be disappointed for a little longer," he stated. " While the test is being carried out, it is not advisable to have you all in the boat— we may require plenty of room. But directly we are satisfied that all is O.K., then the whole troop shall have a run. I require a crew of six, to use the oars if necessary. Saye, Hislan, Raine, Wards, Bell and Elson, fall in aboard the boat. The rest pass in the oars only, then set about collecting all our gear, and see nothing is missing ; we don't want a last minute rush when we strike camp to-morrow."

Without protest, the orders were obeyed, although the majority of the lads were disappointed. But they realised the justness of Mr. Wayte's decision and knew that the chosen six knew more about boat handling than they did. They were also aware that their turn would come later.

Accompanied by Mr. " X " the Scoutmaster boarded the whaler, ordered her to be cast off, and directed the crew to pull her out into the river. Then he carefully wound the starting rope round its groove in the fly-wheel, and, with a word of warning, pulled on the free end. Turned by the unwinding rope, the engine gave two or three throaty barks, but failed to fire properly. Readjusting the throttle and ignition levers, the S.M. repeated the performance. This time he was rewarded with a spluttering roar as the twin cylinders took up their song and the boat began to gather way.

Carefully checking the throttle and spark positions for starting, he settled down to put the craft through her paces under power, opening up and throttling down the engine until he was satisfied as to its capabilities.

Designed primarily to hurtle a " speed-boat " through the water at 25 knots, it propelled the heavier whaler at a good eight knots and, he noted with pleasure, there was no undue vibration and the added stern piece took the strain well and showed no signs of damaging the hull.

"Good enough!" he exclaimed half an hour later. "Now we'll give the whole crowd a short run. Cheers! No one will have to hike home to-morrow after all!"

CHAPTER X

THE MISSING WHALER

THAT evening tea was late and a very simple meal. The whole troop was taken for a trip to the entrance of the river and back and the motor ran without a hitch. No novice at handling engines, Mr. Wayte kept the power unit running easily—he knew the damage that could be caused by over-driving a new motor, and gave the bearings a good chance to " run themselves in." But it was that that caused tea to be late.

Immediately the meal was finished and the utensils washed up, the troop formed up and marched to the Manor. It had been agreed that Mr. Mannaran had given them the engine, and they were going to put their theory to the test and thank him. But to their dis-appointment, they learned that he was absent from home and not likely to return until the following week. They had drawn a blank,

F*

but were saved the possibility of making a mistake in naming Mr. Mannaran as the donor of the engine.

Back in camp, the Scouts played the last rounds of camp games, while Mr. " X " conversed with the Scoutmaster at great length in the latter's tent. Then, after supper, came the final camp fire.

As soon as they were all assembled, Mr. Wayte rose to his feet.

" I have not told you the plans I have made for returning home," he stated. " In fact, until an hour or so ago I was rather in a hole about it, but our good friend Mr. ' X ' has solved the problem by offering his services.

" What was troubling me was getting both the car and the whaler to Portlip. Obviously, I could not do both things alone, and, good as you are afloat after your short course of instruction, I could not let any of you attempt the passage by yourselves, nor could one of you drive my car—these present insurance laws effectively prevent that. However, Mr. ' X ' has volunteered to take charge of the whaler for the trip, and that leaves me free to drive my 'bus.

" I will tow the trek cart as before, but

with a lighter load—much of the gear will pack in the boat. I shall also take three Scouts with me. I am very much afraid the six cyclists will have to ride home—their machines prevent them taking any other course—and the remaining nine of you will form the crew of the boat. Thanks to the motor, I shall have little cause for anxiety from you, for I know Mr. ' X ' will not use the sails if the wind is at all fresh. You have a twenty-five mile run and, taking things easily, should arrive in Portlip long before dark. We leave Bos'n's Wharf at 2 p.m. sharp.

" The names of the drafts will be posted up to-morrow morning after inspection."

Cheers from the whole troop greeted this announcement, even the six unfortunate cyclists joining heartily in—they knew they were exempt from the joys of the sea trip, and the slightly lesser pleasure of a run in the S.M.'s car, but, true Scouts all, they were glad the evacuation problem was solved to the Scoutmaster's satisfaction.

Once again, Mr. " X " kept the troop enthralled by his stirring yarns as the flickering flames of the camp fire grew brighter as the evening darkened and, once more, Mr. Wayte allowed them half an hour's extension of time, but as the clock in the village began to strike ten he gave the order to turn in.

Half an hour later he " made the rounds " for the last time in that camp, remaining a few minutes in each tent to assure himself that all hands had enjoyed themselves and to make certain that they were all comfortable for their last night under canvas. Then he rejoined Mr. " X " in his own tent and talked far into the night.

At 7 a.m. the following morning the camp was quickly astir as soon as the blast of Mr. Wayte's whistle sounded. A rapid swim, before which all blankets and bed-gear were spread out in the sun for a final airing, was followed by breakfast, then every one " turned-to " for packing up. Each Scout secured his personal belongings first, then the tents were cleared, ready for striking. At 10 a.m. Mr. Wayte inspected the camp as usual, and ordered the gear to be packed ready for transport, leaving only the cooking utensils that would be required for dinner.

Tents were taken down and neatly folded. One was stowed in the whaler, in case any

unforeseen occurrence necessitated her crew
staying out all night, while the others were
placed in the trek cart. Each member of
the boat's crew took his two blankets aboard,
as well as his rucksack, and a few provisions
and fresh water were added, the latter being
carried in buckets, with canvas lashed over
the tops, which were suspended under the
thwarts. A journey to the local garage secured
sufficient petrol for the voyage and some to
spare, and by noon there only remained the
dixies to be disposed of.

" What are you going to do with these,
sir ? " asked Saye, indicating the huge pile
of camp-made mattresses, the car shelter and
the screens.

" You can leave the shelter—it's not un-
sightly—but the other things had best be
burnt," decided Mr. Wayte. " Cut them into
small strips so that you won't have too wide
a blaze and go ahead."

The instruction was rapidly carried out,
the whole Troop dancing round the fierce
flames that consumed the tinder-dry bracken.
As Mr. " X " remarked, it seemed a pity to
destroy them—they had been extremely useful—but they could not be left on the vacated

ground ; " leave nothing but your thanks to the owner," was the Scouts' policy.

Directly the last ember had burnt itself out, the ashes were carefully " dumped " in the river, and the turf replaced in the spot where the fire had been. Then the Scouts attacked their farewell camp meal.

This time there was no hour's rest after dinner. Directly it was finished, the cooks' fires were put up, the camp ovens destroyed, and the ground made as shipshape as possible. Then in two lines, extended order, the troop moved across the clearing, picking up every scrap of litter their keen eyes detected, depositing their finds in the refuse hole. Finally, the pits were filled in, unused firewood carefully stacked out of the way in the copse near by and the remaining utensils and tools packed on the trek cart that was already lashed behind the car.

With a sigh, half of satisfaction and half of regret, Mr. Wayte ordered the troop to fall in.

" We are exactly half an hour behind schedule," he announced. " But the splendid way in which you have cleared the ground amply compensates for that. We will now begin to move off—the boat away first. Has anyone anything to say first ? "

" Yes, sir," stated Saye. " We would all like to go and thank Mr. Service for letting us have the camping ground, if that is possible."

" No need to do that ! " exclaimed the farmer's burly voice from behind the troop. He had come through the woods behind them and overheard the Patrol Leader's words. "I'm only too pleased to let you have the ground, and more so since I've seen how well you've cleared up the place. I'm the one to tender thanks—for the way you helped me with the hay ! Now, don't let me delay you with my blathering, but remember, you're welcome to use this place whenever you want to camp again, as far as I'm concerned. I may add, I'll be pleased to see you all again ! "

As he finished speaking, three hearty cheers from the troop drowned Mr. Wayte's reply, but it was evident from the glow on the farmer's cheeks that he appreciated the applause. Then he abruptly turned and plunged into the woods again. The 28th Portlip Troop had made some staunch friends during their stay.

Without any further delay, the heavily-laden whaler was manned and paddled out into mid-stream under Mr. " X's " orders and the engine started up. He had decided to make the trip down river under power as the breeze was heading them, and he decided it was not advisable to tack with so much gear impeding the movements of the crew— a decision Mr. Wayte silently applauded.

With the troop flag fluttering bravely from the masthead and the engine purring sweetly, the whaler slowly gathered way and slipped out of sight round the first bend below the camp, her crew returning their companions' cheers lustily. Then Mr. Wayte ordered the cyclists to move off, following them slowly in his car. Although the party was in a high-spirited mood—they could not be otherwise after their fortnight in the open—there was a feeling of sadness prevailing as they turned their backs on Bos'n's Wharf, which was looking strangely forlorn without the tents and gear that had occupied it for the past fourteen days.

Three hours later the " land contingent " pulled up at the troops' headquarters and unpacked and stowed away the trek cart's

load. Mr. Wayte had kept pace with the
cyclists all the way. Then, with one accord,
they all journeyed to the mouth of Portlip
harbour to see the whaler finish her last lap,
but although there were several yachts and
boats in sight, there was no sign of the troops'
craft.

"Bit early for her yet, isn't it, sir?" asked
Law, who had proudly occupied the seat
beside the S.M. during the journey. "What
speed do you think she will be doing?"

"Perhaps it is," agreed Mr. Wayte. "I
don't suppose Mr. 'X' would be running the
engine very hard as it is new, so five or six
knots would be a fair allowance, I should
say. They've been afloat four hours now
and we have a clear view of five miles to the
point she must round to get here, so we should
pick her up. However, there's no need to
get anxious yet—the motor might have stopped
and delayed them. The best thing we can do
is to cut home for tea and come back in an
hour or so—you don't have to return unless
you want to."

To the Scoutmaster's secret delight, all
turned up again after a hasty tea, but the
time passed without a sign of the missing

whaler, and eventually the watchers **were** forced to give up on account of darkness.

But where was the whaler ?

CHAPTER XI

HOW THE WHALER FARED

"TAKE the helm, Saye," directed Mr. "X" as Bos'n's Wharf was hidden from sight round the first bend. "Keep her just to the left of the centre of the river and don't cut the points too close as you round them. Remember, a heavily-loaded boat like this carries considerable way and would run pretty hard aground if you touched the mud."

"Aye, aye, sir," responded the P.L., taking the vibrating tiller, and settling himself comfortably in the stern sheets, where he had a clear view ahead. Mr. "X" was a sport for letting him steer the boat down the river, he decided. He glanced towards him and saw that, although he was talking to the rest of the Scouts and pointing out various objects ashore and aboard the boat, he was keeping a watchful eye on the course.

Although the engine was running easily,

the boat was passing through the water at a good five knots, but she had a mile an hour adverse current to stem. There was plenty of time, however, and it was better to keep the engine running gently rather than ask for a breakdown by forcing the new bearings.

Already the breeze had dropped considerably and if the power failed it was realised that the crew would have to labour at the oars in the hot sun—a task that did not appeal to any of them.

An hour and a quarter after leaving the camping ground they reached the mouth of the river with its desolate low-lying ground, and headed east across the wide bay between them and Portlip harbour. The open sea was dead calm, with an oily-looking but very slight swell, while the sun blazed down from a clear blue sky. Visibility was not extremely good, for a heat haze had developed since the dying down of the breeze.

Aboard the whaler conversation had practically ceased as she forged ahead against the tide. The crew were happy to be afloat, but drowsy under the stifling rays of the sun. Hislan had relieved Saye at the helm from the mouth of the river and the latter was sitting amidships, peering through a pair of glasses at the distant shore and occasionally seawards. Mr. " X " smoking his pipe was close by the helmsman, keeping a weather eye on things in general.

" Something funny going on on that yacht, sir ! " exclaimed Saye, suddenly, pointing to a small cutter about two miles off the starboard bow. " Look yourself, sir ; I can't quite make things out definitely, but it looks as if they are scrapping aboard ! "

Taking the proffered glasses, Mr. " X " gazed intently for a few seconds.

" You're right ! " he acknowledged, leaning over and opening up the throttle, until the motor was nearly " all out " and the boat rushing through the water at a good eight knots under the extra power. " We must look into this ; head for her, Hislan ! That's no friendly fight, and, in any case, the fools ought to know better than to knock each other about in a small boat at sea ! "

Swept to the westward by the strong tide, the yacht drew rapidly nearer as the whaler tore towards her and details became clearer. As Mr. " X " had said, it was obvious that it was no friendly bout being fought on the

cutter, for the opponents were belabouring
each other heavily. All at once, the larger
of the two struck a blow that staggered the
other and, catching his heel in the low coaming
round the deck, he fell over the side with a
splash, to reappear a few minutes later,
swimming towards the yacht, only to be
beaten off again by a brandished boathook.

Abandoning his tactics, the swimmer made
for the dinghy, towing astern, whereupon
the victor promptly cast it adrift and could
be seen threatening his victim with a sporting
gun he had seized from below.

" Steady, Hislan, steer for the dinghy,"
ordered Mr. " X." " The rest of you keep
down in case any bullets begin to buzz round.
We must find out what it is all about before
we poke our noses in ! "

Within five minutes the two craft were
rubbing sides while the dripping yachtsman,
his face badly battered, scrambled into the
whaler.

" Stop that fellow ! " he exclaimed excitedly,
pointing in the direction of the yacht that
was beginning to forge ahead under the
influence of her auxiliary motor. " He asked
me for a passage across the bay and when we

spotted your boat coming up he took you for a naval craft and set on to me, with the result you saw! I don't know who he is, but he's apparently wanted ashore!"

"Just a minute," interrupted Mr. "X." "You, I take it, own that yacht? You do? Then may I ask are you in the habit of giving a passage to anyone who asks you, even without knowing who they are? You must excuse these questions, but I can't run these lads into danger without good reason."

"That's all right," assented the stranger. "As for myself, my name is James Wiltman— I'm fairly well-known along the coast and so is *Lona*, my yacht. I don't carry passengers as a rule, but this man got a fisherman to put him off to my yacht at Longstone— a tiny, out-of-the-way village about thirty-five miles down the coast—and he begged me to give him a lift across to Dermington, saying his car had broken down, and there was nothing to give him a lift to Portlip station, which was the nearest from which he could get on. As there was a good breeze, I consented. If that satisfies you, may I suggest you get ahead after him, if you are willing to help ? He can only do four knots under power."

" Certainly, Mr. Wiltman," agreed Mr. " X."
" Whack her up, Hislan, and let me take the helm."

The P.L. accordingly opened up the nearly closed throttle—for the outboard motor could not be declutched, but only run dead slow— and relinquished the tiller, Mr. " X " taking it from him.

" The fellow is armed, I believe ? " he asked the yachtsman. " He trained a sporting gun on you, didn't he ? "

" He did, but there's only two cartridges in it, a blank and a shotted one," came the reply. " I was going to replenish my stock at Dermington. Take a chance with that one and he's helpless."

" I wouldn't mind if I was alone," stated Mr. " X." " But I have to remember these lads. We'll do what we can, anyway, even if we keep him in sight until he's forced to put ashore somewhere."

" Thanks," Mr. Wiltman extended his hand and wrung Mr. " X's." " I knew I could rely on you. May I ask your name ? "

" At the present time I am known to these

Scouts as Mr. ' X,' '' answered the temporary S.M. " They are doing all they can to find out my real name, and I am giving them no assistance at all. But that story will keep ; we are picking up on your friend pretty quickly. We must work out some plan."

" Couldn't we rig a blanket between the boathooks and hoist it as a protection, sir ? " suggested Saye. " I've heard that one will stop a bullet if left hanging."

" Try it, by all means," agreed Mr. " X." " Keep well down as well, all of you, in case he shoots. Once he fires the live cartridge, we are fairly safe. Keep those stretchers handy as weapons, we might get close enough to use them." He pointed to the ash sticks that were placed across the bottom boards in notches to enable the oarsmen to get a grip with their feet when at work.

Doing fully two miles to every one covered by the yacht, the whaler came up to her objective fairly rapidly, but it was a long chase. Menacing his pursuers with the sporting gun, the fugitive shouted to them to sheer off as they got within range. It was easy to see that he was desperate, and Mr. " X " was left with a difficult problem to solve. Dare he risk the shot, bearing in mind his youthful crew, or should he just hang around until the yacht was forced to put into port? The Scouts' boat had plenty of food and water aboard, but there was the anxiety of Mr. Wayte and the lads' parents to be considered when they failed to put in to Portlip that evening. Anyway, they couldn't make their home town before dark now, he reflected, and unfortunately there was no other craft in sight that they could ask to join in the chase. For the present they were safe enough with the Scouts behind the stout sides of the boat and the improvised mantlet giving further security.

For nearly three miles the two boats ran side by side, but some two hundred yards apart, although the whaler was cautiously edging closer inch by inch. The situation seemed to be a deadlock; the Scouts' craft hesitated about closing and their enemy cannily reserved his meagre supply of ammunition. Luckily for the pursuers, the flat calm showed no signs of breaking and the yacht's sails hung idle and useless. As things were it seemed that the situation rested on the length of time the petrol supply lasted in each case. Mr. " X " felt thankful when he heard that *Lona's* tanks were of small capacity and knew that the whaler had a fairly large reserve, although her motor required a larger consumption than the yacht's.

" I say, sir," exclaimed Saye, at last. " There's that grass rope we used for mooring aboard. Couldn't we slip across his bows and pay it out ? It might foul her propeller and hang her up ! "

" That's a great idea, by Jove ! " acknowledged Mr. " X." " We'll try it ; move that blanket contraption round as we forge ahead and pay out the rope over the far side when I give the word. Obey every order at once, whatever it is ! "

Assuring himself that there was plenty of fuel in the tank as a precautionary measure, Mr. " X " deliberately opened the throttle wide—for the first time since the motor had been on the whaler. As the roar of the exhaust increased the boat shot ahead until she more than doubled her former speed. Then, well ahead of the yacht, the helmsman turned her to starboard and she shot across *Lona's* bows. At the same time he ordered the grass rope to be paid out over the port side.

"Keep well down and run it through a rowlock," he directed. "I'll tell you when to let go the end."

Like a snake the light warp floated astern of the whaler, Mr. Wiltman keeping it clear of their own propeller with a stretcher. In the meantime their enemy was nonplussed by their manœuvre. Unable to leave his own tiller to go for'ard, he yawed the yacht in an endeavour to see what was happening, but the side of the whaler and the improvised screen blocked his view, while the turbulent "wake" from the outboard's propeller hid the trailing rope from his gaze.

"Let go!" ordered Mr. "X" as he judged that *Lona* was about abeam of the centre of the warp. As the command was obeyed, he swung the boat back on her original course, but this time she was on the other side of the yacht and ahead. Once more the motor was slowed down.

They had not long to wait. Charging ahead, *Lona's* bows caught the rope fairly and the two ends streamed along her sides. The only question was, would the suction of her propeller drag it in sufficiently for the blades to become entangled ?

" It ought to," asserted Mr. Wiltman, answering the unspoken question in Mr. " X's " eyes. " The propeller shaft comes out just under her port quarter and invariably picks up any odd piece of rope in the vicinity, especially when I am in a hurry ! She's got it now ! " he added, as the yacht's speed was seen to decrease. Owing to the sound of their own exhaust, they could not hear the other engine working. " It's stopped the engine all right ; look—the cooling water jet out of the side isn't running ! "

It was so. Not knowing the location of the cooling water exit, the Scouts had not noticed it, but the yachtsman, familiar with his own craft, knew where to look.

Putting his helm over again, Mr. " X " caused the whaler to circle round the now stationary yacht, but still at a respectful distance—there was still the loaded 12-bore to be reckoned with. But now the greater advantage was with the Scouts' craft, yet they were still handicapped by the firearm.

Twice the whaler circled the yacht, drawing slightly closer each minute. Aboard *Lona*, the fugitive was getting desperate, shouting to the Scouts to clear off at once, while he alternately made jabs at the fouled propeller with a boathook and trained the gun on them.

Suddenly Mr. " X " changed his tactics. While some of the Scouts manipulated the blanket screen to protect the length of the boat, he steered slowly towards the yacht.

" You can't get away with it ! " he yelled to the man aboard the yacht. " Give in quietly and save yourself trouble, otherwise we will hang round until you are forced to surrender—we have plenty of fuel and provisions and can outspeed you even if you get a breeze—which seems unlikely. You're properly caught ; show some sense ! "

The answer came quickly in the form of a shot and a volley of oaths. Disregarding the latter, Mr. " X " looked anxiously around the boat following the pattering of the tiny leaden pellets, then chuckled as he saw there were no casualties, and realised that the one live cartridge had been expended.

" We've got him now ! " he exclaimed. " I'm going to lie close alongside, keep him occupied aft, if we can, while some of you board him for'ard. If he goes that end, reverse the attack. Who'll volunteer to board ? You might get hurt, I warn you, but we'll try and get off as lightly as possible."

Without exception, all expressed the desire to be one of the boarders.

" Good ! " resumed Mr. " X " as he steered the whaler round the yacht as before. " I expected as much. Keep your stretchers handy and be ready to use them when the time comes. Don't lower that blanket screen, in any circumstances, until after you hear the second shot from the gun—I know it's a blank, but even a blank can do damage if we are close enough. When we get close enough, the party furthest away from the man will jump aboard and draw him off while the second lot of us boards. Mr. Wiltman will lead the bowmen, I will take charge aft. Smith, you will remain on board this boat—we can't leave her unattended—and prevent any attempt on the part of our enemy at getting aboard and making off in her. All be extremely careful not to trip on the deck or step on a loose rope, or you will be over the side before you know where you are. All understand ? Good ! Then here goes ! "

Bringing the whaler round the stern of the

yacht at a fairly high speed, Mr. " X " headed for the port side. As he anticipated, the fugitive raised the gun and fired point blank at the attackers, unaware that his charge was useless. Considering it was the first time they had been under fire, the Scouts stood the ordeal well, and, before the man realised what had happened, by skilful use of the reverse gear, helm and throttle, the troop boat was brought up within two feet of the yacht's side.

Clubbing his gun, the now desperate man threatened to brain anyone who stepped aboard *Lona* in no uncertain terms, to be jabbed by boathooks in reply, causing him to skip about nimbly to avoid the blows and concentrate on the position of attack.

Taking advantage of the diversion thus created, Mr. Wiltman, followed by Hislan and three other Scouts, jumped on to the yacht's foredeck, armed with their ash staves, and advanced threateningly aft, whereupon the man turned and sprang towards them, making terrific sweeps with his gun butt.

This was the after party's chance. In a trice they too boarded the yacht and rushed towards the scene of the conflict as swiftly as the awkward contours of the yacht allowed, but it was Saye who got in the first telling blow.

Finding himself forced into the cockpit in the rush, he saw his opportunity and ran into the tiny cabin entrance with its pushed-back sliding hatch. In this position he found that his head and shoulders were just clear of the coaming and, furthermore, the fugitive's legs were within three feet of him as he stood at bay on the cabin top with his foes encircling him at a respectful distance. Luckily for him, he had " topped up " the boom until it and the main sail were quite clear.

Gripping his stretcher firmly in both hands, while he braced himself in the narrow companion, the P.L. swung it with all his strength behind the man's knees. Caught unawares by the hefty blow, he staggered and dropped to his knees, his gun slipping from his hands as he did so. Quick on the uptake, Mr. " X " darted forward and brought his own stave down on the fugitive's head without compunction.

The stunning blow ended the fight. Before the man had recovered his wits, he was securely bound hand and foot and placed on one of the bunks in the cabin and the Scouts set about lowering and stowing the yacht's sails, under the direction of Mr. Wiltman, ready for *Lona* to be taken in tow by the whaler.

" Look here," stated Mr. " X," addressing the yacht's owner. " We can't very well leave you drifting about here all night, especially as you have no dinghy and there's little chance of a breeze, so, as I said before, we shall have to take you in tow. Now, we are approximately half way between Dermington and Portlip, and, as I have to get these lads back to the latter port, I propose taking you there. If we're lucky we shall pick up your dinghy before it gets too dark to see it; if not, then I'm afraid you'll have to put up with the loss. I took the liberty of looking through an attache-case down below— it belongs to our friend—and I find it is full of Bank and Treasury notes, which, in view of the circumstances, looks fishy to me. The sooner we place our friend in police hands, the better."

" That suits me," assented Mr. Wiltman. " Thank you all for your help—I should have been in a rotten hole without you. We should make Portlip before dawn, I should think, and the lads' parents will have their fears set at rest sooner than if we went anywhere else at this time of the day—I expect they are getting pretty anxious, as it is."

Within a few minutes *Lona* was in tow behind the whaler, heading eastwards once more. Thanks to the moonlight, the dinghy was located within a few yards of their course and secured without difficulty and just as the rising sun began to show above the horizon, the cortege moved through the narrow entrance to Portlip harbour and brought up alongside the town quay. As the first rope was passed ashore, a familiar figure, its face looking tired and drawn, ran up to them.

" Is everyone all right ? " asked Mr. Wayte, for it was he. " What delayed you ? "

CHAPTER XII

BACK IN PORTLIP

" QUITE all right, sir ! " came a chorus from the boats. " All fit and well ! "

" Yes, we're all O.K., but a bit tired, Mr. Wayte," put in Mr. " X " before the S.M. could say a word. " But we have a few more things to do before we can get away, unfortunately. Is there a policeman handy ? "

" Policeman ? " echoed Mr. Wayte. " What do you want one for—anything amiss ? " he asked, glancing suspiciously at Mr. Wiltman, who was looking somewhat bedraggled in the clothes that had dried on him—no one had stopped to think about offering him a change in the excitement, nor had it occurred to him himself.

" We've got a pretty desperate character lashed up in the yacht's cabin," explained Mr. " X." " We will give you full details later. What about the police ? "

" There's a station not more than a couple of hundred yards down the road—I'll show you, and perhaps this gentleman would like to come too," was the answer. " We must hurry though—these lads' parents are rather alarmed about the delay."

Ten minutes later the three men were at the station, and Mr. " X " and the yachtsman gave the sergeant-in-charge a brief description of the seizure of the yacht by her passenger, their victory over him, and the discovery of the case full of notes.

The sergeant's eyes gleamed as he heard of the latter. " That's the fellow we are after ! " he exclaimed, jumping to his feet. " You've got him safe, you say, sir ? "

" Tied hand and foot in the yacht's cabin," repeated Mr. " X," who had taken charge of the situation. " You'd better send along a couple of men to take him over—he's a tough customer."

" Right, sir ! " acknowledged the sergeant, pressing a bell push and selecting a pair of handcuffs from a drawer as he did so. Almost at once two constables entered the room.

" Come along to the quay with me," he ordered. " These gentlemen have the man who robbed the bank here yesterday morning. Better run the van along—we'll have to take him to headquarters."

After a seemingly interminable wait, the Scouts saw the three men and the police return. Within a few minutes their captive, released from his rope bonds, but securely handcuffed was escorted, hobbling painfully on his stiffened legs and with all the fight worn out of him, to the police van and, accompanied by Mr. " X " and the yachtsman, driven off.

" Good work of yours ! " stated Mr. Wayte abruptly. " Although you did give me a nasty shock when you failed to turn up. However, I guessed you'd come through all right—Mr. ' X ' is to be trusted, I knew. Now, how about it ? Do you feel fit enough to run the whaler round to her moorings ? Three of you will be enough, but two more should stand by the yacht until Mr. Wiltman gets back. Game for it ? "

All signified their willingness. They had snatched a few hours' sleep during the run home, so the S.M. picked out five, including Saye and Hislan, sending the remaining four Scouts to their homes.

Hislan and Wards stood by on *Lona*, while Saye, Raine and Smith, with Mr. Wayte at the helm, pushed off in the whaler for their short run to a small creek that was within a quarter of a mile from their own headquarters. The engine still continued to run well despite its gruelling work and an hour later, the boat having been moored, Mr. Wayte dismissed his assistants to their homes.

But his work was not yet completed. Back he went to the quay to see how the other two were faring, arriving at the yacht at the same moment as Mr. " X " and the yachtsman. They found the two Scouts sound asleep on the bunks, but they awoke as soon as the cabin doors were opened.

" You haven't been long, sir ! " yawned Hislan, rubbing his eyes. " I didn't expect to see you so soon."

" It's just on an hour and a half since I left you," stated the S.M.

" So it is ! " exclaimed the P.L. " George and I just sat down on the bunks and, it seems to me, just dozed off after talking for a few minutes."

" Some doze ! " returned Mr. Wayte. " You two had better cut off home as quickly as you can and get some sleep; I expect you'll have to answer some questions before the day is through!"

"They will!" agreed Mr. "X." "The police want all of us who were in the show to attend at the court at eleven o'clock—it's five-thirty now, so there's not much time. What's the programme now, Wayte?"

"A good hot bath and breakfast for me!" stated the S.M. "I've been up all night waiting for news of you! Care to come along to my place and share those joys? You can turn in, if you like; I'll have to warn your crew about attending the court—luckily I have their addresses. What about you, Mr. Wiltman?" he added, as Mr. "X" accepted his invitation.

"I'll have to see about getting *Lona* on some moorings—can't leave her here," the owner pointed out. "After that I shall stretch out on my bunk for an hour or so. I'll see you all later in the morning?"

"That's right!" agreed the Scoutmaster. "But let us help you get the yacht fixed up. You can't very well manage her single-handed in this tideway without your engine going."

Mr. Wiltman assented with gratitude and

within twenty minutes *Lona* was safely berthed on some borrowed moorings, and Mr. " X " and the S.M. were in the latter's car starting off towards the promised hot baths and breakfast.

Soon after 8 a.m. Mr. Wayte was out again in his two-seater calling at the homes of the whaler's crew, warning their parents that the lads would be required at the police court at eleven o'clock. With one exception, he found that all the Scouts were in bed, fast asleep. That exception was Saye, whose house he visited last. The P.L. was up and dressed ready to go out.

" Good job I caught you, Saye," he remarked. " I've called to tell you you are required at the police court this morning to give evidence against that fellow."

" Good ! " was the strange reply. " I was expecting something like that and just about to call and see you about it."

" Why ' good ' ? " asked the S.M.

" Because, sir, it occurred to me that if Mr. " X " is there to give his evidence, we shall learn his name—it's bound to come out during the proceedings."

" Perhaps," agreed Mr. Wayte. " But

G*

don't count on it too much, you money
grabber ! However, as you are ready to
come out, jump in the car and I will run
you along to the court. We shall be a bit
early—it's barely ten-thirty now—but we can
waste some more time by picking up Hislan
on the way."

They did, and eleven o'clock found the
nine Scouts, the Scoutmaster, the yachtsman and Mr. " X " assembled in the court
for the preliminary hearing of the case.

The accused, Reginald March, was standing
trial on two charges. He had held up the
cashier of a small branch of a bank on the
outskirts of the town and got away, after
seriously injuring the cashier, with £5,000
in notes and silver. It was a big sum to be
in a sub-branch of a bank and in the charge
of one man, but a representative explained
that there had been an unexpectedly heavy
pay in that morning from a nearby firm.
March must have got wind of this and acted
accordingly.

Several witnesses, hurriedly collected, swore
that March was the man they had seen run
from the bank, board a car and drive rapidly
off, and a report from the police at Longstone

stated that this particular car had been found abandoned in the vicinity of the village with a broken driving shaft.

This ended the first part of the proceedings and the court rose for a luncheon interval, but before the Scouts left they saw Mr. " X " approach the magistrate and talk for a few minutes. Mr. Wayte smiled.

After lunch the second charge—that of piracy at sea—was dealt with. Firstly **Mr. Wiltman** described his experiences from the time March asked for a passage at Longstone until he was thrown into the water and picked up by the Scouts' boat. He was cautioned by the magistrate for taking a stranger aboard his yacht and then ordered to stand down.

Mr. " X " then took his place in the witness box. To Saye's disappointment, he still went by the title of " Mr. ' X '," the magistrate explaining briefly to the court that the witness desired to suppress his name for private reasons that were satisfactorily explained to him. " It has no bearing on the case," he added. " Mr. ' X ' desires to remain anonymous on account of a contract he has formed with the 28th Troop of Portlip

Scouts—a contract dating back some weeks."

Once again Saye's hopes were squashed.

Mr. " X " gave a rapid, but clear, account of sighting the yacht, seeing the fight, picking up Mr. Wiltman, the chase and ultimate victory of the whaler and her crew, evidence that was corroborated by each of the nine Scouts in turn, and finally the police sergeant told how he had arrested March in the cabin of the yacht *Lona* early that morning.

It was a long drawn-out business, but by five o'clock the accused was committed for trial at the Assizes and removed to the county gaol to await his trial and the witnesses were warned that they would be required to attend in a month's time.

" I suppose that will mean a holiday from school," declared Wards, as they moved away. " Won't the other fellows be envious ? "

" They probably will," agreed Mr. Wayte, " but you haven't a nice job, let me remind you—it is not pleasing to think you have had a hand in sending a man to penal servitude, however much he deserves it. All the same, I must admit I am pleased with the way in which you fellows conducted yourselves in the chase and with the way you all gave evidence. Well, we've had a tiring twenty-four hours, but I've told the other fellows I'd meet them at the hall this evening. Any of you care to come?"

The full troop fell in that evening at seven o'clock, much to the Scoutmaster's satisfaction. The primary object was to stow and check the camping gear—a task that was best done at once—and he was pleased to see that the Scouts were able to have a heavy day and night and still carry on cheerfully. He expected it of them, but would have quite understood if the younger members of the boat's crew had stopped away. The only absentee was Mr. "X," who had departed immediately after the court proceedings closed.

"Must get away from these reporter-johnnies who will be buzzing round, Wayte," he explained. "Besides that, I have my own work to attend to. I anticipated catching the train last night, as a matter of fact, and here I am, nearly twenty-four hours astern. I'll give you all a look-up as soon as I can; meanwhile, cheer-oh and thanks for your hospitality."

While some of the Scouts worked at the gear already in the hall under Bell's instructions, Mr. Wayte took a party with the trek cart to the creek where the whaler was moored. Then the boat was brought alongside and the remainder of the stores and kit transferred to the cart. Luck was with the Scouts, for nothing had been touched during their absence from the boat and within an hour they were stowing the load with the first lot in their headquarters.

As soon as all was reported correct, Mr. Wayte ordered the troop to fall in.

" So ends our annual camp," he stated. " Taking things all round, I think I can honestly say that it has been a huge success. Besides having a good time, the troop has made some good friends and I can say without prejudice performed two Good Turns of the higher degree—I am referring to your work at the fire and the incident last night. Carting the farmer's hay was just a game and hardly counts. In short, I am jolly pleased with the lot of you. Now, I think, we had better dismiss. I am sure at least nine of you are just as keen to get to bed as I am ! Meetings next week, as usual ! Troop ! Dismiss ! "

" Just a minute, sir, if you don't mind," Saye caught the S.M. as he was about to leave. " Hislan and I would like to have hiking cards to cover the next week or ten days if you can wangle them. We want to do a cycling trip, camping *en route*."

" I'll see what can be done at the Local Association," promised Mr. Wayte. " Strictly speaking, you are hardly eligible as you are not Rovers, but I'll do my best. I suppose this means you'll both be absent next week ? Not tired of life under canvas yet, then ? "

" Rather not, sir," came the reply. " We are intending combining business with pleasure, so we put that forward as an excuse. You see, sir, there's only a little over two weeks before school starts and we promised Mr. ' X ' that he would have to join up before then."

" I see ! " exclaimed the Scoutmaster with a knowing smile. " So that's your game ! May I ask what tack you are working on? It must be pretty definite for you to forego that amount of time in the whaler ! "

" If you don't mind, sir, we'd rather not say anything just at present," put in Hislan. " It's Saye's stunt, but we'd rather report on it after we've done it—successfully or otherwise."

" As you like," agreed Mr. Wayte. " So long as you don't get into mischief. When do you propose to start ? "

" Monday morning, if you can get the permits, sir," stated Saye. " We planned it in the boat last night. If you can get them to-morrow, we'll collect them from you on Sunday and then clear off."

" Excuse me, gentlemen, but may I have a few words with you ? "

They turned, to find the ex-Scout-journalist at the door. " I've been chasing you round all the evening, just missing you at every point. Would you be so good as to give me an account of your adventure yesterday, and, if possible, a few lines on your friend Mr. ' X ' ? He got away before any of us could tackle him."

The two patrol leaders glanced at Mr. Wayte enquiringly.

" Carry on if you like," he assented. " But I'm afraid we can hardly discuss Mr ' X ' without his permission."

" What about you, sir ? Can't you give me the story ? " asked the reporter.

"I wasn't there," pointed out Mr. Wayte. "We broke camp yesterday afternoon. I brought some of the Scouts home by road, while Mr. 'X' was in charge of the others in the troop whaler. They had all the excitement; I had the worry and vigil at this end when they didn't turn up last night."

"That's a pretty good line, at any rate, sir. 'Scoutmaster's lonely night wait for overdue boat.' 'Says was confident that Scouts were safe.' That's right, isn't it? Now perhaps Mr. Saye will give me his side; he was most helpful a week or two ago and I am grateful. May I say that this interview is exclusive?"

Saye laughed. "That seems to be your pet line," he exclaimed. "As regards our affair, there's little to add to what we said in the court this afternoon—I suppose you were there?"

"Surely. But I guess you can add a few personal details to that to make it more in the journalistic line? How did you feel about things when that fellow trained the gun on you and let drive, for instance?"

"None too comfortable," came the admission. "But we were all quite safe.

We knew he only had one live cartridge and Mr. 'X,' who was at the helm all the time, made us all get down in the bottom of the boat where we were absolutely safe. Another thing, we had a thick blanket, loosely suspended between two boathooks, up as a further protection and not one of us was touched when the shot was fired. The boat's sides stopped a few, though. I don't think I can say that any of us was exactly scared —it was too exciting while the scrap was actually on, but we all got fed up when we cruised side by side with the yacht, unable to do anything. Eventually someone suggested fouling the yacht's propeller with a rope. We did it, and then managed to board her and lay out the man. The success of the whole show was due to Mr. 'X.' He handled it all well."

"Thanks, Saye, I'll dish up something with that lot and the court evidence," stated the reporter. "But I wish I could locate that Mr. 'X' of yours."

"We wish we could, too," cut in Hislan, before anyone else could say a word. "We can't very well tell you the details, but he has given us the job of finding out his name

and address by next July, as a test. That
is the reason why he has not disclosed it
to-day. Saye and I are going off in a couple
of days to trail him down, if we can, before
we begin school again—we want to cut his
time allowance down by ten months, if we
can."

"Good luck to you!" came the reply.
"I only wish I was coming with you! That
piece would make rather good news; can I
use it in with the other?"

"I don't think Mr. 'X' would object to
that, if you stick to those details alone,"
decided Mr. Wayte. "On the face of it, it
hardly seems enough to warrant the sup-
pression of his name in the court, but you
can please yourself. Between you and me,
there is little more in the matter. It certainly
is a test for the troop, but it is also in the
nature of a competition between Mr. 'X'
and the Scouts. That, however, is not for
publication. Now, I must ask you to excuse
us; we are all off to bed—we've had precious
little sleep since seven a.m. yesterday.
Good night!"

Mr. Wayte insisted on running Saye and
Hislan to their homes in his car before he

went to his own, and the first thing after breakfast the following morning he went to the Local Scouts Association and obtained the desired hiking cards—" chits " issued by the Scout Authorities giving the possessors their permission to make hike camps where and when they liked, provided the owner of the selected site initialled the cards to denote that he was agreeable.

CHAPTER XIII

THE PATROL LEADERS' MISSION

" 'MORNING, Phil! Ready to start?"
Saye surveyed his uniformed chum
as he opened the door of his home at ten
o'clock on the following Monday morning.

" 'Morning, Bob," came the reply. "So
far O.K., but I think we ought to run over
the route once again before we get going.
Another thing, I want a share of the tent
to pack on my bike. I refuse to let you
lug the whole of the camping gear along
in addition to your own kit, while I have
my rucksack only," he added, looking at
his companion's heavily laden machine, which
carried a small tent, with the necessary poles,
pegs, lines and mallet, as well as billy cans,
ground sheet, light axe and a bag of
provisions.

"Right ho! I don't object," returned
Saye. "But as I didn't know what you

had decided to bring, I pushed it all on my own grid. There's plenty of time for to-day, anyway. Sandshire is just over the fifty mile mark and I think the best thing we can do is to camp for the night just on the border so that we can start work in real earnest in the morning. Don't forget Mr. ' X ' may not be actually in Sandshire itself—the fact that his friend has the Sandshire index letters on his car doesn't guarantee that; he may live in this county, for instance, having bought the car second-hand."

" That's so," came the admission. " But we can only work on the evidence we have at present. At the same time, we should cover a good lot of ground in the ten days we've allotted ourselves. Here's hoping for the best, any-old-how. Now, let's have a squint at the map in comfort before we begin our peregrinations."

Saye assented, realising that his chum was right. They had already discussed several routes, each with its advantages and disadvantages, but no definite one had been decided on. For close on a quarter of an hour they pored over the map, then Saye straightened himself.

" Well, it doesn't make much difference, one way or another, Phil," he stated. " They all cover approximately the same mileage —fifty, in other words—and we have all day to do it in, as we said just now. But, bearing in mind the kit we have to lug along on our machines and the fact that we are ascending hills most of the way, I vote we choose that one," he traced a line with his finger. " We get a pretty stiff climb in the first twenty miles, then it's pretty level for the final thirty."

" I agree with you," assented Hislan. " There's some fine scenery along that way, too, and plenty of camping sites at the end. Now, what about gear ? Have we everything we are likely to want ? "

" Tent, ground sheets, blankets, billies, frying pan, canvas bucket, axe, first aid stuff, swabs, towels, personal gear, soap, mirror, rope, trenching tool, matches and candles," repeated Saye, reading from a list. " That's about everything in that line. As regards the other stuff, we have spanners, tyre lifters, repair outfits, pumps, electric lamps, and I have a spare battery. We shouldn't require anything else to keep our grids going. For to-day's grub and breakfast to-morrow we have one pound of cooked sausages, bread, butter, jam, half a dozen boiled eggs, some rashers and a packet of porridge. Anything else we can buy as we need it."

"That's practically everything," assented Hislan. "But what about tea, sugar and milk, not to mention your mug and plate ? "

"I forgot to mention those, but I packed them all," explained his chum. "Now, for goodness sake, don't think of anything else —there's hardly room for me on my bike as it is ! Come along, we'll just give the machines a spot of oil each and push off— if you're fit."

"O.K.," agreed Hislan. "But I suppose you have some cash ? I only remembered mine at the last minute ! "

"By Jove ! I nearly forgot that ! Carry on with the oiling—you'll find the can in the cycle shed—while I get the necessary. Shan't be a minute."

Hislan obeyed, pausing only to fold up the map with the first section of their journey ready for use and stowing it in his pocket. He had only found the oil-can when his chum rejoined him. Ten minutes later they climbed on to their loaded mounts and started off on their trek. It was just 11 a.m.

They were nearly half an hour getting clear of Portlip and its suburbs ; the roads were congested with traffic and they were held up at a level crossing for nearly ten minutes, but 1 p.m. found them with 18 miles to their credit, and they had a stiff climb in front of them for the next five miles. They were well out in the country, passing through a heavily-wooded district.

" I think it's time we had a bite to eat," suggested Hislan. " There's a pretty decent clearing over there to the right and, unless I'm mistaken, there's the burbling sound of a brook to make it all the more perfect."

" Why should that help ? I didn't know you had a poetic strain ! " responded Saye. " It's not spring, either ? "

" I meant we could get our water from it to make some tea, you silly ass ! " corrected his chum. " You should have realised that ! "

" In any case, I am quite willing to stop." Saye turned his mount as he spoke and made his way back to the clearing that they had overshot while they were talking, Hislan following suite. " A spell-ho, is just what I want," he added, as he brought up by the side of the road, dismounted from his machine and slipped off his rucksack. " I hope there's no law about lighting fires around here, by the way. I don't think this wood is private property, and, in any event, there's no one near that we can ask."

" The best thing to do is to light a small fire to boil the billy just on the edge of the road," suggested the P.L. of the Bulls. " If we stay on the roadside of this ditch I don't see it can hurt. We can move into the clearing when the tea is made and eat our grub there."

" Sound scheme, old man ! " agreed Saye. " Prop the bikes together just on the grass. I'll get the water while you start the fire."

Methodically Hislan collected some small twigs and larger branches of dead wood from the trees in the vicinity, cleared a small patch by the roadside of leaves, long grass and twigs that might spread the flames and started a tiny fire, using the small pieces of wood which he set up in pyramid fashion over a scrap of paper he took from the wrappings of the sausages. Then he added some of the bigger wood, spending his time by improvising a support for the billy over the flames out of a green stick and two forked branches—one to support the first stick at about one third of its length and the other to pin the lower end to the ground. His chum, who seemed to be away a long time, returned just as he finished.

" This would be a wonderful place for a week-end camp, Phil ! " he exclaimed. " The stream is just behind those trees and is fast running over a pebbly bottom and quite clean, besides being beautifully cool. It rises from a spring about a hundred yards further along."

" That part might be O.K.," admitted Hislan. " But this clearing, fine as it is, is rather too close to the road and too open to it for my liking. I know this part of the country is pretty deserted, but you wouldn't want every passer-by to be able to look right in to the camp. Hand me that water and begin to get the grub over to some nice comfy spot. I'll see to the tea."

In a remarkably short space of time the water was boiling in the billy over the deftly tended fire. Measuring some tea leaves into a small net bag that he produced from his haversack, Hislan waited until large bubbles broke the surface of the water and dropped the bag into the billy, which he moved from off the fire. Then he collected his haversack and carried it and the tea across to where Saye was waiting, reclining on a spread out ground sheet.

" Pretty warm, pushing those bikes along," remarked Saye, as he was busy tucking in to the cold sausage, bread, butter and tea that comprised their lunch. " But we've done jolly well so far, considering the load. We shan't do much this afternoon, that's certain. Have you any suggestions for our operations ? "

His chum shrugged his shoulders. " We've run through the details pretty thoroughly and much depends on when we find the farmer who owns car ZZ 99106, and if we sight Mr. ' X ' himself. Neither of these points are certain—it will all be a matter of luck, especially as you couldn't get the name and address of the car's owner. Supposing we do locate Mr. ' X ' on this trip, what do you propose to do ? Are you thinking of going straight to him, or what ? "

" I don't think so," replied Saye. " You see, Phil this is a matter that concerns the whole patrol. If we do succeed and it's up to us to do so, I propose going back to Portlip without saying anything in Mr. 'X's' locality and putting the rest wise. Then, if they like, the whole lot can pay Mr. ' X ' a visit, just as a surprise, or invite him to headquarters to be enrolled."

" That's a fine idea, old man. Let's hope we can bring it off. Just imagine the fellows' faces when we give them the name and address, not to mention Mr. ' X's ' surprise. I wonder some of the others haven't tried some stunt on their own."

" Well, we were lucky enough to pick up the clue of the farmer's car," pointed out Saye. " You must remember that the rest haven't anything in that line to work on, except Law, who found the 'bus in the first place. Smart as he is, I don't think he would try a stunt like this on his own."

" Perhaps you're right," assented his chum. " But remember, in turn, that that Tenderfoot is the smartest youngster we've had in the troop since it started ; he'll be mounting the King's Scout badge before very long, I'll bet. You'll have to look out for yourself then, and so shall I."

" I'll admit all you say, Phil; that lad seems to take to the game like a duck takes to water, but I guess we've gone ahead a bit on this turn-out. Dash it all, man, we've simply got to ! Come on ; time to be moving. Do you realise we've been here an hour and a half ? "

Neatly destroying all signs of their stop, the two patrol leaders repacked their gear, hoisted their rucksacks on to their shoulders and climbed on to their cycles once again, covering the ground easily but making good progress. Barring a halt of twenty minutes for tea at 5 p.m., they did not stop until they found themselves just inside the boundary line of the county of Sandshire at eight o'clock. Five minutes' run down a narrow, winding lane brought them to a snug camping place, far enough from the road to ensure privacy. Here they dismounted and unloaded their machines, then Hislan, carrying the canvas bucket, rode off to find the owner of the land to get permission for them to pitch their tent and obtain sufficient water to satisfy their needs. Saye passed the time by sorting out the gear ready to erect the tent and collecting some wood for the fire.

" O.K.," announced Hislan on his return. " Very decent farmer fellow owns the ground, says we can stay as long as we like. I vote we make this our base for a day or so, while we comb the district all round within a certain radius. Then we can shift and repeat the idea further on."

" Good wheeze ! " acknowledged Saye. " So long as the gear will be all right here. We can see about that later; meanwhile, lend a hand at getting this tent up—knock those four pegs in first; in a square, eight paces between each. I'll get the poles in while you're at it. Then, shove the long guy ropes on the pegs and hand me the ' dollies ' when I'm ready."

Hislan obeyed and, as his chum lifted the canvas shrouded poles and ridge-pole, he deftly slipped the ornamented wooden knob, complete with guys, over the spike of the nearest pole. Then he gently tightened the ropes until they just supported the front end of the tent, while he repeated the manœuvre at the back end. This done, Saye was able to emerge from the midst of the canvas and the pair of them, after lacing up the door in order to prevent any widening of the tent at that end, proceeded to peg out the sides. Five minutes later the billy was being set over a rapidly growing fire.

"What's the menu for to-night, Bob?" asked Hislan, as he squatted beside his friend.

"Bread and sardines," came the decisive reply. "I've got a tin that will just do for the two of us."

"With jam dampers as 'afters,' eh?"

"I haven't either jam or flour in the grub sack, unfortunately. Sorry, Phil, you'll have to be content with the small fish; we must remember to get some flour to-morrow— dampers would be O.K."

Hislan smiled quietly and rummaged in his haversack. "Here you are—shall I make them or you? I felt sure you would forget something and took a chance by bringing this on my own." He produced a linen bag filled with flour and a small pot of jam.

"Well done!" exclaimed Saye. "But a dirty trick not to have told me you'd got it—after all, we did agree that I was to do the catering. To make the punishment fit the crime, you can make the dampers. We'll have the first course while they're cooking."

They did, and had a jolly, well-earned meal in the deepening twilight. Then, having washed up the plates, knives, forks and billycans, they reclined at ease on ground sheets near the fire, talking over the happy time they had all had in the big camp.

"Somehow I prefer this, I think," commented Saye. "But I can quite understand that it might be better in a large camp for a long period. I must say I miss the other fellows, all the same—it seems so quiet here after the buzz of conversation each evening at Bos'n's Wharf."

"That's so," agreed the P.L. of the Bulls. "But it is nice to have a quiet, undisturbed chat over a camp fire after a strenuous day. Don't forget though, we are hardly here on pleasure—we represent the troop on what, I hope, will be a successful mission. As the sole representatives in this district of the 28th Portlip Troop, we have to do ˗ our best . . ." He broke off, listening intently, Saye doing likewise.

" Whee-ou !   Whee-ou ! "   A strange cry came softly through the darkness.

" Strange ! " whispered Saye.   " That is a Widgeon's call, but it doesn't sound quite real to me; besides, I don't think there are any Widgeons around here."

" Rather a coincidence, as you are P.L. of the Widgeon patrol and we were discussing the troop.   I wonder if it will call again," replied Hislan in the same tones.   " Listen ! "

But the evening was still except for the light rustle of the leaves in the faint breeze.

" Probably a stray bird in the vicinity," stated Saye at length, breaking the silence. " In any case, it's nothing to get excited about and I'm feeling just about ready to turn in—how about it ? "

" Sure," agreed Hislan.   " It's about time if you intend to put in a good day to-morrow. Carry on and take those ground sheets into the tent, while I have a final prowl around."

He did so.   All was quiet and, after seeing that the dying fire was quite safe and not likely to set alight to anything in the vicinity, he picked up a small pile of wood and carried it inside the tent—he was not going to risk only having damp wood for the morning. Ten minutes later they were both fast asleep.

At 6.30 the following morning, Hislan slipped quietly from his blankets, picked up his wood and started to make his fire to boil water and cook breakfast. There was sufficient water in the canvas bucket for the tea billy, thank goodness, and a nearby stream, although hardly fit for drinking purposes, was an excellent washing place.

The small, dry sticks burning well, he turned round to the neatly-piled stack of miniature logs Saye had collected the evening before. To his intense surprise and disgust there were only two or three left, and those were scattered—he could have sworn that there was a fairly large pile when he turned in the night before. Perhaps Saye knew something about it, he reflected.

" Wake up, Bob ! " he commanded, shaking his chum's shoulder. " I say," he continued, as Saye roused himself. " Did you touch those small logs last night ? I'm sure there was a whole heap when we went to bed, but there's only a few odd ones left this morning."

" I haven't touched them since I piled

them by the fire site as we were making camp,"
stated Saye. "You did all the handling of
the wood from then onwards. Come and
see if there are any signs of anyone having
been messing around."

There was no doubt that somebody had
disturbed the wood pile, but there was
nothing to give them any clue as to whether
the intruder was man or beast—the thick
grass masked any tracks that might have
helped.

"No use looking at it!" exclaimed Hislan.
"The main thing is to get some more wood
before the fire burns out; it's your turn
to do something, so carry on!"

It was certainly strange; the two Scouts
discussed the matter while they were having
breakfast, but there was no possible solution
that presented itself; it seemed absurd for
anyone to creep into the camp and remove
firewood when there was literally tons in the
vicinity waiting to be collected. At last they
agreed to forget all about the mystery of
the wood for the time, and carry on with
their search—that was the most important
thing of all.

For three days they ranged the countryside,

covering all the paths, roads and byways in an area within twenty-five miles radius from their camp, but there was no sign of either the motor car number ZZ 99106 or any vehicle bearing Mr. " X " amongst its occupants. Their work could only be done by observation and that was a slow business. After all, their main clue was the car and the chances were that its owner would not have it out on the road while they were in the vicinity.

" Three days gone ! " exclaimed Saye, as the two chums were wearily pedalling their mounts up the lane that led to their temporary home. " With nothing to show so far. To-morrow we shall have to shift our headquarters to another part and operate from a spot about fifty miles from here— that allows us our cruising radius of twenty-five miles and allowing for the twenty-five we've done from here. We'll have to start early in the morning to get packed, 'cos we've got to find a new camping ground before this time to-morrow."

" That's so," agreed Hislan. " I hope I shall feel more like it after a sleep—this pottering round does make me feel tired ;

I can hardly push these pedals round ! "

" I feel the same," admitted Saye. " I didn't like to mention it before, somehow. I'd rather do a decent long ride than dawdle round like we have since we arrived here. Rather disappointing, too, not having found anything in the way of clues."

The sound of a motor horn from behind caused both Scouts to crowd to the side of the road to permit a car to pass. It did. Then, to the chums' amazement and delight, they saw, on the rear number plate, ' ZZ 99106 ' !

Making a terrific effort, the Scouts pushed the pedals of their cycles round as hard as they could, but the two-seater eluded them easily.

" Doesn't matter ! " gasped Hislan, as he ceased grinding away. " The fellow in it is the farmer who gave us permission to camp here."

Saye deliberately clapped on his brakes, stopped his machine and dismounted, pulling his chum from his cycle as he did so.

" You utter, silly ass ! " he exclaimed. " Here we've been looking for a man for the last three days and you saw him the evening before that! Why didn't you make sure of things when you first visited the farm and save us all this trouble, you chump? I took it for granted that you had cleared the farm a quarter of a mile away off the list!"

"I should have done," admitted Hislan. "But somehow it didn't occur to me at the time. It seemed quite an ordinary sort of place and I was expecting something quite different, for some reason or another! Well, what's to be done now?"

"Too late for anything but supper to-night," decided Saye. "But the first thing in the morning, we must find out what houses are in the vicinity. Mr. 'X' said his home was 'quite near' to the farm, if I can recollect his actual words rightly. Then it should be fairly easy to find out the names of the owners and fit one on to our friend."

"That sounds O.K.," acknowledged Hislan. "We'll see what happens to-morrow morning."

They did. It was a simple task, for there were only two houses of any size within a radius of five miles from the farm. One was inhabited by two old maiden ladies and in the other " a navy gennelman by the name of Commander Prinket lives there at toimes with 'is sheepdog, but 'e's generally away most of the toime," their yokel informer told them. There could be no doubt; the naval commander with a sheepdog, living in a house called " The Wardroom," could be none other than their Mr. " X."

" Cheers ! " exclaimed Hislan, when they gained the news. " What are you going to do, Bob ? Call on him now, or stick to our original plans ? "

" Start off home at once ! " decided Saye. " If we get going without any delay, I guess we shall be in time to catch the other fellows at the hall before they shut down for the night—they're sure to be there to-night."

By dint of furious packing and hard cycling, aided by the down slope of the country, they managed to enter Portlip at seven o'clock that night. They had been slightly delayed at the start by the farmer, who had asked them if they had enjoyed their camp and, to their surprise, referred to Bos'n's Wharf in comparison. But they were in time to catch the rest of the troop, at any rate.

Parking their loaded cycles in the entrance, they burst into the large hall, ready to give all the scouts the good news. But before they could utter a word their companions did a curious thing. With one accord they cupped their hands over their mouths and roared :—

"His name is Commander Prinket!"

CHAPTER XIV

THE TENDERFOOT'S TRIUMPH

TENDERFOOT LAW watched the two patrol leaders speaking to Mr. Wayte a little grimly. It was hardly fair, he reflected, for them to keep him out of the last lap, especially when he had done the dirty work at the Redley Garage. He was positive that they were arranging for a trip into Sandshire. Well, he would go, too, if his friend didn't let him down. Saye and Hislan were jolly decent fellows; there was no doubt about that, but, like all the bigger fellows at school and everywhere else, they didn't like youngsters hanging around too much, except when they could make them useful in some way.

Law did some deep thinking as he walked homewards that night. By Jove, yes! He would show them! He quickened his pace and turned abruptly off the course that led towards home—luckily it was still early. An hour later he confronted his father in his study.

"Well, what do you want, son?" demanded Mr. Law, as his son entered the door. Things were apparently well for Law Junior, for when his father used that detestable "son" as a form of address it usually meant he was in a good mood.

"Will you let me go on a cycling camp for two or three days next week, please, Dad?" he asked. "I've got that small hiking tent and all the other stuff."

"Bless my soul, you've only just come back from a fortnight's camp," exclaimed Mr. Law. "Haven't you had enough?"

"No fear, Dad!" came the reply. "Not only that, but two of the big fellows are going and I want to show them I can do it just as well as they can."

"I don't see why you shouldn't go then," agreed his father. "When will you start?"

"Monday morning, early, I hope, sir."

"Right you are then, son. But mind those other fellows don't tire you out—they are bound to be able to do more than you can."

With a final word of thanks, the Tenderfoot

(not troubling to enlighten his parent regarding his mistake in believing that his son was going in company with the two patrol leaders) went to his mother and gave her ample notice for the procuring of the necessary food and gear he would need. She had no objection to raise, being under the same misapprehension as her husband. Then he got busy with his own plans.

Early on the Monday morning he was up and busy loading his gear on to his cycle. His outfit was scanty, but sufficient for his needs—he had merely tent, blankets, ground sheet, billy and sufficient food tinned and cooked, to last him at least 48 hours. Then, after an ample breakfast, he mounted his cycle and pedalled out on to the shortest road to Sandshire.

At noon he stopped at a clearing and consumed his lunch. He did not stop to make a fire to boil water for a drink, but risked drinking from the spring that was in the vicinity. Then he tidied away every sign of his meal and stoppage and resumed his journey—a bare half-hour in front of Saye and Hislan, had he, and they, known it.

It was a long and lonely ride, but the

Tenderfoot did not notice it. Regularly he reeled off the miles, keeping up a steady average of 8½ m.p.h. except when he stopped for lunch and tea. He had plenty to think about. The scenery around him was enough to keep him interested in the normal course of events, but now he had the excitement of his mission to keep him occupied and the question whether Saye and Hislan were ahead of him or behind, on the same road or some other ? Had they the same information as he had or not ? It was only time that would answer them.

It was close on 6 p.m. before Law drew up at some cross roads and looked around in doubt. He was somewhere near his objective, but how near ?

" Catslip Varm, sur ? Sure, you takes thikky lil' lane down along thur and thur she be," explained an ancient yokel when he asked the way. The directions were ample, although crude, and a few minutes later the Tenderfoot was leaning his machine against a gatepost of Catslip Farm. It was only a few moments' task to find the farmer himself, and Law had no difficulty in recognising him as one of the people he had seen in Redley on the day he raided the garage. So far, so good.

"Certainly you can put your tent anywhere you like around here," replied the farmer in answer to Law's request. "You'll find an ideal spot just up there behind the house. Follow that footpath and you will find it without trouble."

"Thank you, sir," acknowledged Law. "But there's one more thing, if you wouldn't mind. There are three of us around this district and the other two might be along before long; I should be very much obliged if you did not mention the fact that I am here to them if you see them. You see, they don't know I am on this trek and I want to beat them at it if I can."

"Right you are; I'll keep quiet," promised the farmer. "But what exactly is this trek you are on? Surely I saw you during the week before last at Redley? I believe your troop was camping at Bos'n's Wharf, wasn't it?"

"Yes, Mr. Berner," replied Law, the name slipping out, much to the Tenderfoot's confusion. "We were there until last Thursday. This trek is just a stunt of our own—

we wish to find some information in this district."

" I notice you've started already by learning my name ! " exclaimed the farmer, who struck Law as being a retired army man by his general bearing. " How did you manage that ? "

Law decided to make a clean breast of it ; it seemed the only thing to do. " I saw your car in Redley when we were looking for clues to establish the identity of a gentleman who has been very decent to us," he began. " I thought at first that it was his car because of some dog's hairs on the cushions —and he had a dog with a similar coat—so I copied the number—ZZ 99106, it was. Later on we found that the gentleman's car was not in the vicinity, but he saw you and said you were a neighbour of his, so I went to an A.A. Scout that I know and he told me that car ZZ 99106 was owned by A. Berner, Esq., of Catslip Farm, Sandshire. I got that news last night and came along here to-day. I would rather you did not tell me our friend's name, sir—I mean to find out on my own."

" That is extremely interesting," acknowledged Mr. Berner. "May I ask the next step you intend to take? I don't intend to 'queer' you in any way, but I am rather interested, for I happen to know your Mr. 'X' pretty well."

"That's why I made for this place," pointed out the Tenderfoot. "Once I located your farm I knew that Mr. 'X's' home would not be far off. To-morrow morning, as soon as I know where the other two are—if they have chosen this route, and I'm inclined to believe they have—I shall have a look at the houses round about, find out the names of their owners, see them if I can manage it and run Mr. 'X' to earth. It should be very easy, I think, sir."

"The best of luck, anyway," responded Mr. Berner. "Now you must excuse me— I have a little job needing my attention. If the others do turn up I'll keep mum about you. Good night!"

Thus dismissed, the Tenderfoot moved off along the indicated path and soon found a camping site that appealed to him. Working quietly, he soon had his tent pitched and everything comfortable and shipshape. Then he prepared and ate his supper, feeling somewhat lonely on his first solo camp. He almost regretted having reversed his first idea and not asked one of the others to come with him. Then he steeled himself—he'd bring this stunt off single-handed, he vowed.

Although it was beginning to get dark he did not feel at all like sleeping. Another thing, he wondered if Saye and Hislan had come the same way into Sandshire—he would have a careful look round and see.

Carefully skirting the farm, he followed the lane up which he had cycled earlier in the evening, keeping well in the shadow of the hedge and moving as noiselessly as he could. Barely a quarter of a mile from the farm he smelt wood-smoke—the same as he had learned to know and appreciate while at Bos'n's Wharf—it was perhaps the P.L.'s. ?

He paused and noted the direction from which it was coming. Slightly to the right. Good! There was also a small wood and a stout hedge over there—excellent cover!

Five minutes later he was gazing at a small tent, dimly outlined against the flickering light of a small fire, and the silhouettes of Saye and Hislan as they yarned in front of the fire before turning in. So they had come the same way! But how much did they know? That was the question.

For a fleeting moment he considered making his presence known, but he speedily ruled that out—perhaps he still had a chance to win on his own. Instead he would give them something to think about! That was the idea, but what? Suddenly he raised himself a trifle and, cupping his hands round his mouth, he uttered his patrol cry: " Whee-ou!   Whee-ou! "

The two patrol leaders stopped talking and looked about them, trying to locate the position from where the sound came, but Law kept absolutely quiet, although he was chuckling to himself with glee. For some minutes his victims remained silent and in a listening position, then they resumed their yarns, the Tenderfoot remaining, with infinite patience, quietly in his hiding-place—why, he couldn't definitely say, for he was out of hearing distance of ordinary conversation and there was not sufficient cover for him to risk going any closer, despite the dark.

Before very long he saw the two making preparations for turning in. First Saye disappeared into the tent, then Hislan, after taking up some wood and carrying it with him. But more was left in a neat pile by the dying fire, Law noticed, and it gave him an idea.

Allowing five minutes to elapse after he saw the candle in the tent put out—five minutes that seemed like hours—the Tenderfoot crawled silently over the intervening ground, his heart bumping with suppressed excitement at each step. But at length he was within reach of his objective—the pile of small logs.

Whipping off his scarf, he quietly piled the sticks on it, tying the two ends over the lot when he had removed all but two or three. Then he retreated as he had come, carrying his load, which he scattered in the small wood as he passed through. Half an hour later, he, too, was asleep in his own tent.

At six o'clock the following morning he was awake. He possessed the pleasing faculty of being able to awaken at any time he wished, and had settled on 6 a.m. as giving him sufficient time to be in his position to spy on the other two before they were about.

Stuffing some bread and a tin of sardines in his haversack, he set off and, snugly bedded down on his ground sheet, he contentedly munched the food while he waited for Saye and Hislan to appear.

The latter was first and he began to light the fire, carefully setting the small dry sticks he brought from the tent. Soon they were burning well and he looked round for the bigger fuel. Then the watcher saw him bound into the tent, to reappear a few minutes later with Saye and point to where the small logs had been piled the night before.

They cast around for several minutes trying to pick up tracks, much to the amusement of the Tenderfoot, who knew what marks he had made in the grass would have disappeared during the night. He had certainly "got the P.L.'s. guessing" and would have something to pull their legs about when they all returned to Portlip, whether he was successful in finding Mr. "X's" name first or not.

Doggedly he stuck to his self-imposed task of watching the other two until he found out what they were going to do. He could not risk starting off on his own errand and run into them; his job was to keep clear if he could. At last the patrol leaders cleared away their breakfast things, straightened their gear, lashed the door of their tent and went off on their cycles. It was obvious that they were going fairly far afield, for they carried haversacks of food and light cooking utensils. Law nearly hugged himself for joy when he saw this—Saye and Hislan had missed the clue that was right under their noses, unless they knew something else that he didn't— anyway the morning would show.

Returning to his own tent, the Tenderfoot washed and changed into full Scout uniform, tidied up and marched off on his own business, following the tracks of the two cycles from their camp into the nearby village. Here, Law noticed with relief, they passed straight on, whereas his interest was quite close by.

Feeling in his pocket to assure himself that he had some money with him, he made for the one shop the village boasted of. He knew by experience that these tiny general stores could supply every bit of local gossip and information in addition to the usual shop stock; that he had learned at Redley and other villages during holidays—this place should be the same, especially if some old dame was the proprietor.

Such was the case, he found, when he entered the low, timbered shop. A few small purchases and the goodwill of the white-haired old countrywoman was secured, then a carefully chosen remark released a flow of conversation that Law turned easily into local channels. Within fifteen minutes he had heard the names and habits of the most prominent people in the village itself and then his informant started on the " gentry," as she termed the residents of the big houses.

" And then there's that there Commander Prinket up at ' The Wardroom,' " the flow continued. Law pricked up his ears ; this sounded like his quarry. " He's a strange gentleman, with a strange name to himself and to his house. But he's a good sort and not at home as much as we would like— us villagers, I means—but I do hear that he travels about all over the country in his motor car and last Saturday I see his photograph in the newspaper—he had caught some bank robber it said."

The Tenderfoot was pretty sure of his

ground now ; in fact he had all the data he required—it had been singularly easy to get, too—but he wanted to make sure that Commander Prinket and Mr. " X " were one and the same if it were possible. " Which bank robbery was that ? " he asked, " and what is Commander Prinket like ? I may have seen the picture myself."

" I expect you did," agreed the old lady. " It were the robbery at Portlip. They said that our Commander was with some Boy Scouts in a boat when he caught the thief —you must have seen it, young fellow. They called him Mr. ' X ' in the paper 'cos he didn't want his real name know'd—like the real gentleman he is. He's tall and wide, with grey hair and generally wears those baggy short trousers—what they uses for golf. You couldn't mistake him if you seed him, but you won't 'cos he's gone away for a day or two, they tells me."

There was no doubt of it ; Mr. " X " and Commander Prinket were one and the same person, Law was certain. General as the description was, it was good enough to make him recognise Mr. " X " from it. Thanking the shopkeeper politely, the Tenderfoot made his escape and hurried back to his tent. If he hurried he could easily make Portlip by that evening and so avoid any danger of being seen by Saye or Hislan in the vicinity and get Mr. Wayte to send off the " notice of discovery " to Mr. " X " before they returned.

Calling at Catslip Farm on the way, Law thanked Mr. Berner for letting him have the camping ground and told him he was returning to Portlip that day.

" Been successful in your quest already then ? " asked Mr. Berner. " You've been mighty smart if you have ! "

" I am pretty certain, sir," replied the Scout. " Your general storekeeper supplied me with full particulars of practically everybody living around here—I only had to draw my own conclusions."

" I see ! " exclaimed the farmer with a laugh. " With such detail as she gave you could hardly make a mistake ! Am I to tell the other two you were here, or keep quiet ? "

" Keep quiet, if you please, sir," responded Law. " I just want to see how long they take on their own and give them a surprise. Good-bye, sir, and thank you ! "

With the majority of the hills in his favour, the Tenderfoot made light of the journey and arrived at his home early in the evening. Pausing only to dump his camping kit, he cycled round to the hall, where he expected to find most of the troop and Mr. Wayte. He did.

" Excuse me, sir ! " he exclaimed, addressing the Scoutmaster. " May I speak to you a moment, please ? "

" Carry on ! " directed Mr. Wayte. " I'm listening."

" I have just found out Mr. ' X's' real name, sir ! " reported the tenderfoot. " He is Commander Prinket and his address is ' The Wardroom,' Catslip, Sandshire. I have just come from Catslip this afternoon—I located Mr. ' X's ' name and address this morning. Will you write to him and ask him to come over, sir ? "

" You're quite sure you've not made any mistake, I suppose ? Saye and Hislan started off yesterday on the same quest, but I've not heard anything from them so far. Tell me how you found all this out."

Without hesitation Law told his story from the time he raided the garage at Redley to his farewell conversation with Mr. Berner, omitting nothing. Mr. Wayte listened intently.

"Very interesting," he stated, when the Tenderfoot had finished. "Furthermore, I think you've managed jolly well and I will send a line to this Commander Prinket. I don't know Mr. 'X's' real name myself, so I can't say whether you're right or wrong. If you are right and Saye and Hislan are not back before we know definitely we'll give them a big surprise as a reward for not seeing what's under their nose, as it were. Now I'll tell the rest—hang on a moment."

The Scoutmaster's announcement was received with three ringing cheers and the Tenderfoot had a warm ten minutes from his delighted fellow Scouts. Then they set about planning the patrol leaders' reception for when they returned.

Thursday morning there was a letter from Mr. "X," acknowledging that he had been found out and asking when he should come to Portlip to see them. "Don't forget I promised you all a good day at my place if you found me at home," he added. "It's up to you now."

It was agreed that they would enrol Commander Prinket—or Mr. " X," as they preferred to call him—before any other plans were made. Meanwhile there was the matter of Saye and Hislan to be dealt with. Each evening since the Tuesday a look-out had been posted to give warning of their approach so that the troop should not be caught napping.

The following morning, just after the last Scout had turned up at the hall, the sentry cried out that Saye and Hislan were coming along on cycles. According to plan, all the lads grouped themselves facing the door and, as it burst open to admit the excited P.L.'s. they yelled in unison—

" His name is Commander Prinket ! "

The result nearly exceeded their expectations. Saye and Hislan stopped dead in their tracks as if they had been shot. Then, before they had fully recovered " Whee-ou, Whee-ou ! " the troop chanted. " What became of the small logs for Tuesday's breakfast fire ? Ask Law ! "

Quick to grasp the significance of the words, Saye strode forward, blushing hard, and wrung the Tenderfoot's hand heartily.

" How did you do it ? " he asked. " You certainly whacked Hislan and me at the game ! "

In a few words Law gave his version of the hunt to the genuinely pleased P.L.'s. They bore him no grudge and openly acknowledged that they had " asked for it."

" When do we rope Mr. ' X ' in ? " asked Saye. " We'll make him pay for all this ! "

They did the following week.

THE END